THE COLLAR

Evelyn Allen Harper

Ink Smith Publishing
www.ink-smith.com

Evelyn Allen Harper

ISBN: 978-1-939156-59-4

Ink Smith Publishing
710 S. Mrytle Ave Suite 209
Monrovia, CA, 91016

The Collar

Preface

Susan Cook, a residential real estate agent, had no reason to believe that her customer, Charles Holiday, was anything but an ordinary buyer. Charles was neither ordinary nor a buyer; he was a man running for his life.

Ryan Wilcox, a professional golfer, had exposed a ring of gamblers who were injuring athletics to ensure the outcome of a game. The head of the syndic issued a high-paying contract to the person who would kill Ryan. He was found in a northern Michigan town where he had been hiding for ten years.

Susan Cook was the person Ryan ran to for help. While fleeing his enemies, the plane Ryan was piloting crashed in an isolated area. The survivors of the crash were Susan, Ryan, and a fur coat he had given Susan before the flight. The coat was their only protection against the elements. Huddled together under the coat, love blossomed.

Ryan's enemies found him. Susan and the coat returned home. Ryan was considered dead to everyone but Susan.

Black depression from what she called the *Incident* kept Susan sitting on her front porch, bundled up in Ryan's coat. Things changed when an invalid moved into the house across the street. For as long as the invalid lived there, Susan's dreams were wonderful love-filled ones.

Chapter 1

Coffee.

Wide-awake, Susan Cook watched the luminous numbers on the digital clock across the room change from 2:17 to 2:18 A.M.

Damn coffee!

Yes, Susan, her inner voice chided her, *decisions do have consequences. Caffeine is not your friend.*

With a resigned sigh, she fluffed her pillow, pulled the covers around her shoulders, and closed her eyes. It was going to be a long night and she had no one to blame but herself. Just because everyone at the table had ordered coffee with their dessert, did that mean she had to order it, too? Groaning, she pounded the pillow and kicked off the covers. Never again! Even while she was drinking it, her inner self was screaming at her. So why did she? Maybe she could blame her lapse of good judgment on peer pressure? With that amusing thought, she relaxed. There was still a smile on her face when sweet, elusive sleep was creeping…what was that noise?

Without moving, her eyes flew open. Across the room, the numbers on the luminous digital clock changed from 2:30 to 2:31 A.M …and then the face of the clock disappeared.

She blinked. The clock reappeared, still showing 2:31 A.M. The hair on the back of her neck stood up. Even though every nerve in her body was screaming to move, she forced herself to remain motionless. Someone was in her room.

Fear-filled time passed in silence until her anxiety rose to an explosive level. Leaping out of bed, she flipped a switch filling the room with light. After checking under her bed and inside the closet, she ran through the house turning on lights.

Her pounding heart was the only sound that filled her ears as she checked the locked doors and shut windows. While passing her front window, the lighted house across the street caught her attention. Light from the open front door was spilling out over a white-coated attendant who was pushing an empty wheelchair down the ramp. One by one, the lights in the house went out, plunging it and the surrounding area into complete darkness. The van backed out of the driveway and drove away.

A much calmer Susan turned off lights as she walked through her house one more time. Satisfied that she was alone, she crawled back into bed and fell into an uneasy sleep.

The jarring morning alarm woke her. The fact that her sleep had been absent of dreams didn't hit her until after she silenced the noise. Memories of wonderful dreams were the fuel that gave her strength for the day. Feeling empty, she tried to pull memories from the past to fill the void; it didn't work.

The warm bed and the quiet house were lulling Susan back to sleep when the memory of the clock incident jarred her awake. Had she imagined it, or had there been someone in the room standing between her and the clock?

She jumped out of bed, ran to her bedroom window, and looked at the house across the street. An invalid lived there. For weeks after he moved in, his attendant had pushed his wheelchair to the front porch in the morning. She had sat on her porch swing and imagined paying him a visit. But she never did. Her breath caught in her throat when she remembered the empty wheelchair. Had the invalid died?

She watched the house for a few minutes hoping to see some kind of activity. There was none. After promising herself that later today she would cross the street and ring the doorbell, Susan turned away from the window and headed for the shower.

***

Susan Cook, a residential realtor, looked up from behind the front desk at Town and Country Real Estate as Denny McCain walked in.

"Good morning, Denny!" she called to the tall, broad-shouldered, handsome young man. "How's the brand new real estate agent this morning?" Denny had passed his real estate exam with flying colors on the first try.

"And good morning to you, too, Mrs. Cook," he grinned at the blond, blue-eyed, and very attractive woman he was planning to make his mother-in-law. "That test was a piece of cake!"

"Sure, it was," she remarked with a sarcastic note in her voice. "You have to remember that I once took the darned thing."

Flashing his white smile and winking an eye, he teased, "Okay, to you I will admit the test made me sweat a bit, but you can't tell your daughter I said that!"

"Okay, I won't."

"Promise?"

"I promise. But tell me, what's it like to work in the only real estate office in town that uses a dog as a greeter?"

Denny laughed. "Lucky is such a great dog. He sure brings in a lot of business."

Susan nodded. "I know that's true. I've lost customers to that office because of the dog."

Denny looked around. "Hey, who says this office couldn't have a dog of its own? Granted, this isn't a big office, so it would have to be a small one."

"Enough of this," laughed Susan. "Am I right to think you have a buyer and you're here to pick up a key to show one of our listings?"

Denny made a face. "Don't I wish!"

"It will happen, Denny, but it takes time."

"Thanks for the encouraging words, but that's not why I'm here. Are you aware that there's a barking dog in your new listing on Green Street?"

"A dog? But the renters moved out three days ago! Don't tell me they left their dog behind!"

"Looks like it. The neighbors are complaining about the noise. What's the story behind the house?"

"The original owners have been long gone and now the bank owns it. It was one of the houses that your dad pretended to own, advertised it for rent in out-of-area newspapers, and collected the first and last months' rent of the unsuspecting renters who moved in."

Denny cringed. "Even though he's in prison, his foul deeds live on!"

"Do you hear from him?" Susan asked.

"Not a peep, and I'd like to keep it that way. The last time I talked to him he kept trying to make me say I was sorry that I'd shot him. I'm not, and I won't say that I am!"

"And you shouldn't have to!" Silence descended on them and Susan could feel Denny's discomfort. She knew he hated talking about his father, but since Denny was dating her daughter, she felt she had the right to ask questions.

Susan cleared her throat. "Well, back to the dog thing. I'm on floor duty for another half hour. Why don't you stick around and go with me when I check my listing?"

"I can do that," Denny agreed. "I'll be back in thirty minutes. Since we might need a leash if we have to catch the dog, I'll go buy one at the pet store."

"Good thinking!" Susan said as she picked up the ringing phone. "Town and Country Real Estate, how may I help you?"

Denny left the office grinning. He had just scored points with his future mother-in-law.

CHAPTER 2

A moving van was parked at the curb and a crew was hauling furniture out of the house next door when Denny and Susan pulled into the driveway of her listed house. They had just climbed out of the car when a rough-looking man with several days' worth of hair-growth on his face exited the house next door and headed toward them.

"You better be here about the damn dog!" he called over the distance between them. In the background, they could hear incessant barking coming from Susan's listing.

Susan threw up her hands. "Sir, I just heard about the dog a half hour ago. My number is on the sign that's in the front yard. If you were so upset, why didn't you call me?"

"Don't get lippy with me, lady," the man snarled. "You're no better than the hillbilly renters!"

"Did you know them? Do you have any idea why they would leave a dog behind in a locked house?"

"Maybe they didn't like the ugly little rat. I sure don't! I was going to throw a brick through the window and let the asshole dog out, but my wife wouldn't let me. She said it wasn't fair to let anything that ugly run loose in the neighborhood. I'm just glad we're moving."

Denny raised his eyebrows. "A dog is making you move?"

The man glared at him. "I was transferred, smartass!"

Denny took a step toward the man. "Smartass?"

"You heard me!" the man snarled.

Denny's hands rolled into fists.

Susan turned her back on the neighbor, grabbed Denny's arm, and jerked him toward her listing. "Just ignore him!" she whispered into his ear.

Denny didn't move.

Alarmed at the threatening look on the man's face, Susan hissed, "Denny! Drop it! Right now!"

The neighbor was still glaring when Denny turned and followed an amused Susan. "You men! Always trying to prove you can lift your leg higher than the other guy."

Denny's laugh was explosive. "Mrs. Cook! I can't believe you said that!"

She grinned.

Denny was now more determined than ever to marry Susan's daughter.

They could hear the dog barking and scratching on the other side of the door. Denny stopped Susan before she turned the key in the lock.

"The dog is going to run out as soon as you open the door."

Susan nodded. "You're probably right. What do you suggest?"

"Just open the door a few inches and I'll reach in and try to snag him. If he has a collar, it should be easy. If not, well, he just might slip through my hands. He's probably hungry and thirsty."

"Oh, drat!" Susan grimaced. "I should have brought some dog food! I wasn't thinking."

"Are you ready to open the door?"

"Ready!"

It took just a few inches of open space for the dog to stick his head through.

Susan gasped. "Denny! Close the door!"

"I can't close the door on its head!"

"This is a dog? I've never seen anything like it in my whole life!"

"We both heard it bark, so I'm pretty sure it's a dog."

"But what kind of a dog? It's so ugly, it's almost pretty!"

They could see that it was small, but it was so frantic to get out of the house Susan was having trouble holding the door.

"Grab it!" she yelled.

"There's a collar! Got it…I think!"

Holding onto the dog, Denny pushed his way into the house. "Get in here and shut the door! I can't hold it much longer!"

Following Denny's instructions, Susan rushed into the house, pushed the door shut behind her…and tripped over Denny who was sprawled on the floor. There was no sign of the dog.

Regaining her balance, Susan wailed, "I thought you said you had it."

Looking chagrinned, Denny pulled himself into a sitting position. In his hand was an ornate dog collar.

"Did you see where Houdini went?"

"Houdini?" Denny raised his eyebrows.

Susan called from the kitchen. "The dog's not in here. Did you see which way it ran?"

"I don't think the dog went upstairs. Let's hope it stayed on this level."

Denny pulled his head out of the hall closet in time to hear Susan's voice coming from another part of the downstairs.

"Oh, you are the best! Yes, you are!"

Her wannabe son-in-law grinned. He was pleased that Susan was saying nice things about him.

"Mama's gonna take care of you, yes she is!"

Denny's grin disappeared. "Uh, Mrs. Cook, are you talking to me?"

Susan laughed. "Don't you wish? No, Denny, I'm not talking to you. I found the dog."

Denny was glad she couldn't see his red face. "Where?"

"In the laundry room. It wedged its body behind the washing machine. I'm trying to coax it out."

Following the sound of her voice, Denny's rush into the laundry room came to an abrupt stop when he got a good look at the creature that had crawled out of its hiding place. With a quick intake of breath, he stepped back and rubbed his eyes.

Susan laughed. "Rubbing your eyes won't make the dog any prettier."

Accepting its fate, the animal sat down and quietly surveyed its captors.

"Who is it looking at?" wondered Denny.

"It's hard to tell," Susan sounded puzzled. "I think there's something wrong with its eyes."

"Looks like it."

"Hmmm."

 "Wonder why its tongue sticks out like that?"

"Hmmm."

"Mrs. Cook, what's with the 'Hmmms'?"

"I was just trying to remember if I'd ever seen an uglier dog than this one."

Denny grinned. "I must admit that it would never win a beauty contest, but it seems like a nice dog." When the dog held up a paw, Denny stooped down and shook it.

"See what I mean?"

Susan didn't answer because she wasn't there.

"Mrs. Cook?" Denny called.

"I'm in the kitchen," she yelled back. "I imagine there are piles to clean up, but there are none on this level. Stay with Strabismus while I check upstairs."

Denny's mouth dropped open. "Strabismus? You've named the dog Strabismus?"

 Susan glanced back over her shoulder as she climbed the stairs. "Look it up, Denny," she laughed.

"There are no accidents up here," she called down. "Do you think the dog is so housebroken it was able to hold everything for several days? For Heaven's sake, Denny, take it outside! Poor thing!"

The dog stood patiently while Denny replaced the collar. Once the leash was hooked, he opened the door and followed the animal's lead to a grassy area. He thought the dog was giving him a "Thank-you" look, but since the eyes were going in different directions, it was hard to tell.

Locking the door behind her, Susan stepped out. "Everything okay?" she asked.

"Seems to be. By the way, Strabismus is a he. What now?"

"I'm glad you're with me, Denny. You can stay in the car with the boy while I do some shopping."

"Shopping?"

"Dog stuff. You know, bowls, food, dog shampoo, brush…stuff like that. He does have a collar, but maybe I should buy him a new one while I'm there."

Denny took a closer look at the collar around the dog's neck. It looked as if it were handmade.

"I've never seen a collar quite like this one, seems heavy, but I don't think you have to buy a new one." Denny turned to Susan and raised his eyebrows. "Mrs. Cook, are you keeping the dog?"

Memory of the vanishing clock was as scary in the daylight as it had been in the middle of the night. It was as if someone had walked in front of it but she wasn't about to tell Denny why she was thinking about keeping the animal.

"Could be!"

"I suppose it's lonely in your house with Julia gone most of the time."

"Come on, Denny! My daughter isn't there because she spends all her time with you!"

Denny's face turned a bright red.

Susan elbowed him. "I'm joshing you, Denny. I'm happy Julia found someone like you." She paused to swallow a lump in her throat. "We should all be so lucky."

12

The Collar

Don't go there…don't go there! Susan's inner voice yelled at her as she opened the car door.

The dog sat in Denny's lap for the short ride to the pet store.

"I'll be right back," Susan said as she got out of the car and slammed the door. She didn't hear the dog's mournful whine, but Denny did.

The dog jumped off Denny's lap, stood on the driver's seat, and watched Susan disappear into the store. His body remained still until the door of the store opened and Susan, her arms full of packages, walked out. The dog's whole body came alive, his tail wagged, and the noise that he made sounded musical.

Susan opened the back door of the car and threw her purchases onto the back seat. Seeing that the dog's tail was wagging wildly, she grinned. "I'm glad I'm back, too. Now, move over."

The dog moved over to allow Susan into the car. She was pulling into traffic when he stood on his hind legs, laid his cheek against hers, and purred like a cat.

Denny laughed. "Mrs. Cook, I think Strabismus has adopted you!"

CHAPTER 3

Julia Cook, first-year teacher, prayed that Principal Sheldon wasn't around to see her last eighth-grade class push, shove, and chase each other out the door. No matter how much she planned, and no matter how hard she tried, she couldn't consistently control her classes. A momentary lapse of her concentration, a few seconds of relaxed attention, or a weak spot in her presentations was all it took. Trying to regain the upper hand left her perpetually exhausted.

Her thoughts went back to the very first day of the school year. How grown-up she had felt, standing by her open classroom door, waiting for the sound of the bell that would signal the beginning of her teaching career. A woman hurrying down the empty hall had caught Julia's attention. When it became apparent that she was heading for her room, Julia plastered a huge smile on her face. Her college professors had stressed the fact that a good teacher is one who engages the students' parents in the educational process.

The woman, ignoring Julia's outstretched hand and welcoming smile, had swept past her, stuck her head into the room, and looked around. Not finding whom she was searching for, she had turned back to Julia.

"Honey," she had said. "I need to speak to your teacher."

Julia remembered how deflated she had felt. True, she was young, and by the time students reach the eighth grade, some of them were as tall as she. That first day, in order to differentiate herself from her students, she'd worn her blond hair in a neat French twist; it hadn't worked.

The problem had carried over to her classroom. What did she have to do to make her students view her as an adult, not as a friend?

Today, for example, she had raised her voice, threatened the entire class with detention if things didn't improve, and declared that no one should even think about leaving their seats until the dismissal bell had rung. The familiar feeling of defeat washed over her when Elizabeth got out of her seat, walked to the front of the room, and hugged her.

"Ah, Miss Cook," she cooed. "You are so cute when you get angry!"

Julia sat alone in the empty classroom feeling overwhelmed, defeated, and fatigued. Failure was a word that had never before entered into any phase of her life, but if today was an example of her teaching capabilities, then that's what she was. The tears she had been holding back all day were running down her cheeks when the phone rang. It was Denny.

"Hi."

"Kids gone?"

"Yes."

Just by the sound of depression in her voice, Denny knew the answer, but he asked the question anyway. "Another bad day?"

She sighed. "Is there any other kind? Whatever made me think I could teach?"

The daily erosion of both her sense of humor and energy was painful for him to watch; he hadn't heard her laugh in days.

"Don't be so hard on yourself, Hon! Eighth graders are a tough bunch! Could it be you chose the wrong age group to teach?"

She snorted. "Meaning what?"

"I hear fourth-graders are much nicer to their teachers than eighth-graders."

"How do you know that?" Her voice was flat. "You've never taught fourth grade."

Denny laughed. "No, I haven't, but stick with me, Babe! I have answers to all your problems."

Julia grunted.

In a teasing voice, Denny asked, "Wanna play a guessing game?"

"Denny, cut it out! I'm tired, and no, I don't want to play a guessing game!"

"Ah, come on! Humor me!"

Julia sighed. "Didn't you hear me say that I'm tired? I just want to get out of here and go home."

"Well, then I guess you don't want to know that the ugliest dog in the world has adopted your mother."

"What?"

Denny laughed and hung up.

Julia hit speed dial.

Exhaustion forgotten, she exclaimed, "My mom? Come on, now! My mom isn't even a big fan of animals. You can't drop a bomb like that and hang up!"

"I just did," he chuckled, feeling relieved that he'd helped to get Julia into a better mood.

"Denny," she laughed, "quit teasing! What's going on?"

A much more serious Denny answered the question. "The renters in your mother's new listing on Green Street moved out and left a dog locked in the house."

"No!" she breathed. "No one is cruel enough to do that!"

Denny said a thankful prayer to whoever might be listening. If Julia could survive after what his dad had done to her and still be naïve enough to think that bad things didn't happen, it was nothing short of a miracle.

"Well, they did. Your mom and I went over there after neighbors complained about a barking dog. We'd left my car at her office, so after she dropped me off, she was heading home with the dog."

"That sounds so unlike my mother!"

"She's already named it. It's a strange name. When I questioned her about it, she told me to look it up. She calls him Strabismus."

Julia was quiet for a minute. "Does the dog have crossed eyes?"

"Well, yes. There is something wrong with his eyes. How did you know?"

"That's what the word means. You said he was ugly. How ugly is he?"

"How ugly is he, you ask?" Denny chuckled. "Since actually describing the dog would require words that I don't have in my limited vocabulary, I think I'll let you see for yourself."

Julia rolled her eyes. "Come on, Denny. Quit exaggerating."

"Just keep that accusation in mind when you get a look at the dog, and then you can apologize to me the next time you see me. By the way, are you eating dinner with your mom tonight?"

"Why do you ask? Do you have other plans for me?"

"You know I do," he replied in a husky voice.

"Sounds like you have after-dinner plans," Julia chuckled.

"Always."

"Let's talk about dinner. I'll call mom to let her know I'm stopping at the store and picking up something to cook. Shall I tell her that you'll be joining us?"

"Will that be okay with your mom?"

"You know it will. Meet you there?"

"We have a date."

Julia sat quietly for a moment after she ended the call. Teaching was not for the faint of heart, but with Denny's support, maybe she could make it to the end of the school year. His pointing out that teaching fourth grade would be easier than teaching eighth grade was an interesting thought; it was something to consider.

She was about to gather her things and depart for the day when a movement caught her eye. All the students and most of the teachers had gone home long ago. Had someone just peeked around the open door to her room?

When she closed the door to her room and locked it, the hall was empty. She must have been imagining things.

CHAPTER 4

Julia paused for a second before opening the door to her mother's house. The laughter that she heard coming from within was an unusual sound, one that she hadn't heard very often since the Incident. In fact, there were two very different sounds. One was her mother's laughter, and the other was a rather strange, nonhuman, musical noise.

Since she knew her mother wasn't aware that there was an audience, Julia quietly watched the little show. Her mother was in deep conversation with a strange looking dog. She could see why Denny hadn't tried to describe the animal. Just telling her that the rescued dog was ugly hadn't prepared her for what she was seeing; Julia was speechless.

Every time Susan's voice went up at the end of a question, the dog cocked his head to the side and answered her with a melodious howl that involved at least an octave of musical notes. After each performance, Susan laughed until tears ran down her cheeks. Finally, she looked up and saw her daughter.

"Oh, Julia!" she cried, wiping her eyes. "Look what I have!" Susan blew her nose. "Oh, honey, I haven't laughed like this in a long time."

Julia nodded. "I can see that! Denny says you've named him Strabismus."

Susan stroked the dog's back. "Yes, the poor little thing is cross-eyed."

"Mom, how do you get him to make that funny noise?"

"That's singing, Julia! My dog is singing!"

"Sure he is, Mom." Julia stepped closer for a better look at the dog. Except for whatever it was sticking out around his head, the dog was hairless.

Susan cuddled him and cooed. "You're mama's little baby, yes you are! Locked up for days in that old house, you must have been so scared. Mama's not going to let bad things happen to you anymore. No, she isn't! Mama thinks you're the cutest little…."

"Mother, stop that!" Julia yelled.

Susan looked up. "What?"

Strabismus sang a series of notes that seemed to harmonize with each other.

Julia looked at the ugly cross-eyed singing dog and started to laugh. Susan joined her, and soon mother and daughter were laughing so hard they were holding each other for support.

"Whoa!" Denny exclaimed, walking into the living room. "Whatever it is that the two of you are smoking, I want some!"

Julia sobered up enough to talk. "Denny, ask a question, just anything to make your voice go up at the end of it."

He looked puzzled. "This some kind of English test?"

Strabismus didn't even look at him.

"Do it again."

"Do what again?"

"Ask another question."

"Another one? What was the first one?"

"Denny, listen up. You asked if this was some kind of an English test. That was a question. Now, ask another one."

"You're pulling my leg, aren't you?"

The dog paid no attention to the conversation.

Susan and Julia looked at each other. "Do you think it's just female voices?" Julia asked.

The dog got up and walked over to his drinking bowl.

"He didn't react to you, either," Susan observed. "Do you think it's just my voice that causes him to sing?"

Strabismus whirled around, threw back his head, and sang a line of notes.

"Oh, now I see what you were trying to do! Mrs. Cook, didn't I tell you when you got into the car after shopping at the pet store that Strabismus had adopted you?"

"Yes, you did, Denny." Susan looked thoughtfully at the dog that had walked back to her. "I don't know how I feel about being owned by a dog."

Denny sniffed the air. "Uh, I was invited to dinner, but I don't smell anything good coming out of the kitchen."

Raising her eyebrows, Susan looked at her daughter, opened her mouth, and then closed it. "I was about to ask a question," she remarked. "I'm going to have to learn to make statements instead of asking questions. It's obvious that my owner has an opinion about my voice."

Her owner looked up at her with love in his crossed eyes. While scratching the back of the dog's head, Susan stated. "Julia, I hope you remembered to stop at the store on the way here."

"I did. Denny, would you please get the groceries out of my car?"

Parked in Susan's driveway were two very different cars. Julia's car was a sweet red convertible that her mother had bought her last Thanksgiving. Celebrating her independence along with the first year of teaching, Julia had moved out of her mother's house and was living on her own. After the Incident, Julia had moved back in with her mother.

His car, on the other hand, was a wreck. Half of the time, it wouldn't start. When his dad had been around, Dennis Senior could usually get it started, but his dad was in prison. Denny had helped put him there.

Grabbing the groceries out of the trunk of Julia's car, he carried them into the house. The cross-eyed dog greeted him at the door.

After dinner, Susan and a recently bathed Strabismus watched the couple leave to go to Denny's home. It was really his dad's house, but with his dad incarcerated, Denny lived there alone...except when Julia visited.

Her house, always felt so ponderously quiet when Julia left, felt as if it were crushing her. Opening a closet door, she pulled out a huge fur-lined fur coat and carried it with her outside to the front porch swing. The fall air was nippy and the coat felt warm against her skin.

With the clean-smelling dog on her lap, Susan sat huddled inside the coat. Memories came to her of the months following the Incident when she had spent hours on the swing, staring at the house across the street. An invalid, who had moved in sometime after she had returned home, was wheeled out most days to sit on his porch. The two of them had never spoken to each other. While the weeks after the Incident were rough on Susan, she'd found that after the invalid moved in and was on his porch, she felt quite peaceful. As long as he lived there, her dreams at night were wonderful.

Her thoughts went back to what she had seen last night. It bothered her that the wheelchair had been empty when it was put into the van. Had the invalid died? She had wanted to cross the street so many times, but something had held her back. Dare she go now? For some reason, having Strabismus with her gave her the courage to snap the leash onto his collar and cross the street.

The house was dark, but then she thought it would be. The few windows that she was tall enough to peek through didn't show anything but a furnished house with no occupants. Susan felt disgusted with herself; she should have made the trip across the street months ago. Now it was too late.

With her head down, her flight back to the comfort of the swing came to an abrupt halt when Strabismus stopped to smell something on the neighbor's sidewalk.

"Oops!" she exclaimed, regaining her balance. "You and I had better set up some walking rules before one of us gets killed. I almost stepped on you!"

The dog kept sniffing. "What did you find that smells so good?" she asked the dog who replied with just three notes.

Stooping down, Susan picked up the object.

There was still enough daylight for Susan to see what Strabismus had found; it was one of her old business cards. She stood with the crumpled and soiled card in her hand and remembered that her new cards had been on her desk when she'd returned to work after the Incident. The only difference between the new and the old card were the C.R.S. initials after her name; the initials stood for Certified Residential Specialist. She had attended classes and passed exams to attain that title. Puzzled as to why one of her old cards would be on this side of the street, she stared at it until the dog pulled on the leash.

"Aren't you going to help me solve the mystery?" she asked the dog who seemed anxious to keep walking.

Strabismus hummed.

Susan put the soiled card into her pocket and let the dog pull her back across the street to settle again on her swing. She didn't go into the house until it became too dark to see across the street.

Since there was nothing on television that caught her attention and she had finished all the books that she'd hauled home from the library, there wasn't anything left for her to do but go to bed. That's when she remembered that as a dog owner, she was now responsible for the well-being of a living and breathing creature. Slipping the leash onto his collar, they made a trip outside. Strabismus knew exactly what was expected of him.

The dog watched her intently as she got ready for bed. He made no move to join her until she was settled. Then, with a quick jump, he landed lightly next to her, put his nose under the covers, and tunneled in. Straightening himself out, his head emerged from under the covers to rest itself on the extra pillow.

With a feeling of contentment, Susan sighed and buried herself into the soft blankets as she smiled to herself. If you'd ask her, she wouldn't have been able to tell you why the ugly little dog made her feel so safe. He just did.

She was looking forward to sleep. She couldn't remember when or why they began, but for sometime now, her dreams had been filled with sunshine, laughter, and the memory of loving a wonderful man.

With Strabismus at her side, she had quite forgotten that there had been no dreams the night before.

CHAPTER 5

The next morning, Julia was sitting at her desk, dreading the bell that would send the first group of eighth-graders pushing and shoving into her room. If today was no better than yesterday...no, she didn't want to think about it. Filling her head with thoughts about the mess that she was making of her first year of teaching was no way to start the new day. Today just had to be better. Her lesson plans were precise, today's quiz was self-explanatory, and the homework assignment had been laid out in exact steps.

The bell had not yet rung but already she could hear a commotion outside her closed door. With a big sigh, she shrugged in resignation. Today was not going to be different from any of the other days. Leaving her desk, she was making her way to the front of the room when the bell rang, the door flew open, and two boys, locked in an embrace, fell into the room. Fists were flying, blood was squirting, girls were screaming and the other boys were cheering on the fighters. The final blow fell when

Principal Sheldon pushed her way into the room that had suddenly become as quiet as a church.

"Have you no control over your class, Miss Cook?" she thundered.

Silence.

"Well, Miss Cook, have you nothing to say for yourself?"

Julia's first inclination was to cry. Tears started to fill her eyes at the unfairness of it all. Her principal had stepped into the situation and decided at a glance that it was her fault. Something told Julia that there was a choice to be made right here and right now that would make or break her teaching career.

Raising her head, her eyes were filled with sudden determination, her voice rang strong. "Class, I want every one of you to find your seat immediately. No talking."

To her amazement, the class obeyed. Turning to the boys who had picked themselves off the floor, she said, "You two will go with Mrs. Sheldon."

She heard Mrs. Sheldon snort.

"Mrs. Sheldon, I really don't care what you do with the boys. You can call their parents, you can keep them after school, and you can punish them. I don't wish to see their faces in any of my classes for the rest of the day. Good day, Mrs. Sheldon."

Turning her back on her principal whose mouth was hanging open, her eyes moved from one student to the next, daring any one of them to misbehave. There was something new in her eyes, something that told the class that things were different now.

The three morning periods progressed so smoothly that Julia was surprised to look at the clock on the wall and realize it was lunchtime.

She was also surprised that the morning had actually been fun. Maybe she hadn't chosen the wrong profession after all.

"Line up," she ordered. "Wait for the bell, and no running in the hall. Remember that a lot of you have gym class the first period this afternoon."

Julia watched as her usually unruly students lined up quietly, and at the sound of the bell, did exactly what she'd told them to do. Would wonders never cease? That's when she noticed that Amelia wasn't lining up with the rest.

"Something wrong?" she asked the girl.

Amelia was never one of her problem students. She was so shy Julia hadn't had any reason to pay much attention to her. As the girl walked toward her, Julia noticed that she was moving stiffly, looking as if walking were painful. The girl handed her a slip of paper.

Julia unfolded the note and frowned. "Amelia, you asked to be excused from gym last week, too."

Amelia hung her head and spoke so quietly, Julia had trouble hearing her.

"I didn't hear what you said, Amelia. Would you please say it again, only a little louder this time?"

"I fell, Miss Cook."

Julia looked her over, and not seeing any obvious injuries, she asked, "You fell? Did you break anything?"

The girl shook her head.

"As I remember, last week you asked to be excused from gym because you weren't feeling well."

"I...I...I was sick," the girl stammered.

28

"Last week you seemed to recover right after the rest of the class returned from gym. Amelia, is there something you'd like to talk to me about?"

Amelia looked at the floor. She'd been hanging around Miss Cook's room trying to work up enough nerve to approach her. This was her chance, but did she dare?

"Amelia?"

The girl used her foot to trace a soiled spot on the floor. No matter how much she wanted to, she just couldn't do it.

"Amelia, I'll ask you again. Do you need to talk to someone?"

She raised her head, looked into Julia's eyes, and answered. "No."

"All right, then. You know the drill. Give the note to your gym teacher, and you will spend the hour in the principal's office. Take your books with you so that you'll have something to do."

Amelia's eyes dropped back to the floor. "Thank you, Miss Cook."

Julia spent her free period polishing the afternoon lesson plans. When the hour was up, she greeted the returning class with a smile. They, with the exception of Amelia who brought up the end of the line, smiled back.

The girl was definitely having trouble walking.

CHAPTER 6

Susan opened her eyes that morning to find another set of eyes wandering over her face. Briefly shocked, it took her a few seconds to realize that it was her new dog.

"Good morning, Strabismus!" she cooed. "Did you sleep well last night?"

The soft question was worth four of the dog's musical notes.

Susan laughed. "You are going to be so goo...." She stopped. The realization that, once again, there had been no dreams last night wiped the smile from her face. She needed those dreams. Without those dreams, her life was colorless. Without those dreams, life wasn't worth living.

Directly after the Incident and before the dreams began, she had lost the will to survive in a loveless world. She'd retreated from all outside contacts, refused help, stayed in bed, and was content to drown in her own misery. And then the dreams had started. She hadn't questioned why at the time, but now she did.

Closing her eyes, she curled into a fetal position wondering what had caused the change. She just knew that one morning she had awakened feeling wonderful. The crippling dark depression had been replaced by the memory of a wonderful dream. Her eyes flew open; she remembered.

It was the morning after the invalid had moved into the house across the street. But why would that be? It had to be just a coincidence.

But if it had been just a coincidence then why, now that the invalid was gone, had the dreams also left and the black feeling returned?

She needed those dreams. It was the dreams that had fueled her days. It was in anticipation of the dreams that sent her to bed each night. In her dreams, she lived gloriously with the man she loved. In her dreams, the man loved her back as intensely as she loved him. In her dreams, she was a whole person, a desired woman and an eager lover. Her real life, in contrast, was void of the wonderful things that made the dreams special.

Her descent into the familiar pit of despair was cut short by an ugly cross-eyed dog that was forcefully poking his nose into her curled body.

"Cut that out!" she ordered.

Being a good dog, Strabismus quit poking and switched to digging.

Annoyed that her misery was being interrupted, her voice was stern. "You crazy dog! What are you trying to do?"

The dog answered her questions with a line of notes.

Susan's face relaxed; just looking at the dog made the day brighter. Climbing out of bed, she headed to the kitchen to start the coffee. Strabismus had other ideas. He ran to the door and scratched.

"I'll bet you need to go out, don't you?"

If the amount of notes were any indication, the answer was affirmative.

She looked down at her bare feet and short gown. "Can you please wait for me to get dressed?"

After the dog sang what would amount to one verse and the chorus of a long song, Susan gave up, hooked the leash to his collar, and headed out the door.

While waiting patiently for Strabismus to take care of his business, she happened to glance across the street where the invalid had lived. A moving van was in the driveway, and a crew was carrying furniture out of the house. A sudden feeling of loss swept over her with such intensity she shivered.

The dog nudged her leg and headed for the door. He knew that breakfast had to be somewhere and he was going inside to look for it.

Susan scooped dog food into Strabismus' bowl, poured herself a cup of coffee, and leaned against the kitchen counter to watch him eat. He sure was a funny little thing. Leaving a dog behind in a locked house was a heartless thing to do. Maybe someone was supposed to pick him up after the bank kicked the family out of the house. Dennis McCain Senior, who was currently cooling his heels in prison, probably would remember the name of the tenants from whom he had collected the first and last months' rent on a house that he didn't own.

However, Susan was not about to ask Denny to talk to his dad. Until fallout from the Incident opened his eyes, Denny, who had believed that his dad wasn't much different from any other dad, was embarrassed, shocked, and horrified to discover that his dad was very different. His dad was evil. She knew it was hard for Denny to think of his father that way, but after he'd heard him give the order to kill Julia, he'd confessed that those words still managed to make their way into his nightmares.

The Collar

Strabismus licked the bowl clean, looked up at her with wandering eyes and then sat down to scratch at his collar. Since she had seen him doing this several times, it occurred to her that maybe there was something about the collar that was bothering the dog. When she had removed it before giving him a bath, she'd noticed that it was a heavy collar for such a small dog. Along with the other supplies, she should have bought him another one. If he continued to scratch, that's what she'd do.

The black mood that had been lightened by the funny dog came back in full force after she drained the last bit of coffee in her mug. Laying her head on the counter, she closed her eyes and felt the energy drain out of her body. Forgetting about a shower, forgetting about work, she slowly made her way back up the stairs to her room. The unmade bed looked inviting; she crawled back in, pulled the pillow over her head, and went back to sleep.

There were no dreams.

It took just one look at what the school's cafeteria was serving to make Julia decide to go home for lunch. Knowing that there was leftover spaghetti from last night's dinner made the decision easy.

As she drove by the pet shop on the way home, she remembered her mother mentioning that Strabismus' heavy collar seemed to annoy him. The lunch break was just one hour, but grabbing a lighter collar wouldn't take much time. Parking on the street, Julia ran into the store, grabbed and paid for a small blue collar, and within minutes was back in her car heading home for the leftover spaghetti.

When she arrived, she was surprised to find that her mother's car was still in the garage. Susan had told her that she'd be working with a transferee in the afternoon and needed several hours of preparation time before the buyers walked into the office of Town and Country Real Estate.

Using her key to open the door, she walked into a quiet house. For several months after the Incident, Susan had spent most of her days either in bed or on the front porch swing wrapped in the coat. A trip upstairs and a peek into her mother's room confirmed her worst fear. She had tried countless times to talk her mother out of the black moods but nothing she said ever made any difference. With a disappointed sigh, she turned to walk away. Julia stopped when the lump on the other side of the bed came to life. She watched Strabismus crawl out from under the covers and, although his wandering eyes made it hard to tell, she was fairly sure the dog was looking at her.

All she had to say was, "Hi, Strabismus, wanna come and see what I bought for you?" and the dog jumped off the bed and followed her down the stairs.

Julia picked him up, placed him on top of the counter, and removed the heavy collar from around his neck. When Strabismus gave her a kiss on the cheek, she chose to believe that it was his way of saying "Thank you."

Removing the new collar from the box it came in was another matter. With words best left unspoken about the sadistically evil person who had encased the collar in layers of impossible packaging, she was beginning to fear that the lunch hour would be over before she even had the chance to eat the spaghetti. In desperation, she opened the junk-drawer and found a pair of scissors. Once the collar was liberated, she put it on the dog.

"There. Isn't that better?" she asked.

His tail wagged wildly in answer.

Unnoticed by dog or human, the dog's tail swept the old collar off the counter and into a crack between the counter and the stove.

Chapter 7

It was past midnight when a car pulled into the driveway of the house on Green Street. The headlights flashed over the FOR SALE sign in the lawn before being extinguished. A lone figure got out of the car, made its way to the side door, opened it with a key, and disappeared into the house. The house remained dark except for light emanating from a flashlight that moved from room to room.

The light went out as the side door opened. The figure came out and got back into the car.

"Is this your idea of a joke? The dog's not there!" the figure barked into his glowing cellphone. The blue light cast the man's features in an eerie color as he listened.

"I know...would you listen? I said I know I was supposed to pick him up yesterday."

The man listened to the person on the other end of the line.

"Things happened. I'm here now, so where's the dog?"

He listened.

"I don't think you fully appreciate your situation. Should I remind you?"

He listened.

The man's hand tightened around the phone in his hand. "No, I haven't forgotten that you have been very cooperative up to this point."

He listened.

"Yeah, yeah, I know you love your wife."

He listened.

"That is not acceptable! Do I have to mention your daughter?"

He listened.

The man's voice rose, "Wait a minute! You are the only other person who has a key to the house! So don't give me any more of your shit!"

A light came on in one of the nearby houses and the man took a frustrated breath.

"Did I see what?"

He listened.

"The house has been put on the market?"

He listened.

"You say you told me that was going to happen?"

He listened.

"Okay, okay. I messed up."

The man peered off into the yard, squinting. "It's too dark to see it. What does the sign say?"

He listened.

"You think she might have the dog?" there was a long pause, "Do you have this Cook woman's address?"

It was dark in the room when Susan finally forced herself to open her eyes. She sat up, threw her legs over the bed, and stretched. Even though she had slept most of the day, the realization that there had been no dreams sent her back into a dark funk. In a moment of self-pity, she lay back down on the bed. While reaching for the covers, her hand encountered a furry head.

"Strabismus!" she exclaimed! "I've forgotten about you!"

Sitting up, she reached out and pulled the dog close. "What is this around your neck?"

The dog tilted his head and trilled several notes.

"A new collar! I'll bet Julia came home for lunch, didn't she?"

The answer sounded more like a gargle than musical notes.

"I'll bet she ate the leftover spaghetti, too," Susan muttered under her breath as she and the dog descended the steps. Even though Susan had not dressed for the day and was still in her nightclothes, she hooked the leash around the dog's new collar and ventured out into the yard. Night had slipped up on her and it was with regret that she thought about the lost day. By allowing herself to indulge in self-pity, some other salesperson, probably Zena, now had her transferee. A sense of guilt swept over her. It wasn't right that without her commissions, they were living mostly on Julia's paychecks.

Her thoughts were elsewhere, so when Strabismus became intensely interested in something behind a juniper bush, the leash easily slipped out of her hand. The next thing she heard was a yelp, the slamming of a car door, the rev of an engine, and the awful noise of tires squealing as a car sped away.

The Collar

Susan rounded the bush with her heart in her mouth. As she feared, there was no dog.

CHAPTER 8

In another part of town Amelia was stretched out on the floor, her ear close to the grate over the hot-air vent. The room directly below her bedroom was where her father met with men that she never saw, only heard. Her dad's voice was harsh and she could visualize what his face looked like. Since a kick or a fist usually followed that tone of voice, she coiled her body out of habit. Very seldom did he touch her face with his fists; he beat the parts of her body that would be hidden by clothes.

It was late and Amelia's eyes were getting heavy. Almost asleep with her head on the register, the sound of the doorbell roused her. Whoever was at the door did something or said something that agitated the men. With her ear on the register, she was trying to understand what they were yelling about, when the yelp of a dog startled her. Amelia's eyes flew open. Why would the men be bringing a dog to her father? He hated dogs.

When the yelp turned to an incessant bark that caused the men to talk louder, Amelia could clearly hear what they were saying. Apparently, the dog that was presently barking non-stop was supposed to have a different collar around its neck.

The next things she heard were the howling of a dog and the slamming of the front door. Then, from outside, she could hear the sound of the dog whimpering. She hadn't seen it, but she knew what had happened. Her dad had kicked the dog and then threw it outside.

The voices in the room below became full of anger, accusations, blame, and denial. The sound of the whining dog was ignored.

She knew what the dog was feeling; she had felt the brunt of that foot many times. What if she sneaked outside and rescued the dog? With all the noise the men were making, chances were that no one would hear her.

The house was large with a back staircase that led directly into the kitchen. Back when her mother was alive, the servants used the back stairs to enter into their work area without encountering family members. There were no servants now. Amelia didn't understand it all, but it had something to do with her mother's wealthy family. The parents were right in not approving the marriage of their daughter to a man who thought more of using his fists and feet rather than his words to make a point. When she died, the funds from her parents that had been flowing into the union dried up. Unfortunately, Amelia looked nothing like their beloved daughter. If she had, maybe they would have treated her differently. But she didn't, and they had very little contact with their granddaughter.

Using the back staircase, Amelia left the house. Even though the night was dark, the sound of the whimpering dog made it easy for her to locate it. Relieved when she saw that it was a small dog, she inched toward it with her open hand in front of her praying that the scared dog wouldn't bite her. The sound of the front door opening paralyzed her. She'd been caught! Holding her breath, she didn't move until she saw that it was just her father's visitors leaving. It also meant that she had run out of time. Throwing caution to the wind, she scooped up the dog and ran for her life back into the house. She went up the back staircase, taking the steps two at a time, and into her room. When she was securely inside, she took a couple of deep breaths before taking her first real look at the animal she'd rescued.

Amelia swallowed hard. Looking back at her was the strangest, ugliest dog she had ever seen. Trembling, the frightened dog huddled in her arms.

Something was wrong with her father. He had no right to inflict pain on others just because he was bigger. The hate that she felt toward him for hurting the defenseless dog was greater than it was after one of her own beatings.

She had been crying along with the injured dog, but suddenly the reality of what she had done dried the tears in a hurry. She couldn't protect herself, so what made her think she could protect a dog?

The dog had fallen asleep in her arms. He looked so peaceful she hated to wake him to see how badly he was injured. So instead, Amelia crawled into bed, pulled the covers over both of them, and went to sleep.

She'd worry about it in the morning.

Julia stood by the classroom door, welcoming her first-period eighth-graders. Whatever had happened yesterday had carried over; the raucous behavior of the past was gone. She breathed a sigh of gratitude.

Julia's eyes scanned the room. Everyone was present and accounted for except Amelia. A few seconds before the last bell, Amelia, carrying a case, scurried into the room and took her seat.

It wasn't until near the end of the period when noise coming from the case caught her attention. Curious, Julia got up from her desk, walked down the aisle to where Amelia was cowering, looked into an opening in the case, and jumped when one eye, quite crossed, looked back at her.

"Amelia, please see me in the hall…immediately!"

The frightened girl burst into tears but stopped in the middle of a sob when the classroom door opened and a uniformed police officer entered the room.

Julia was caught with her arm outstretched, a finger pointing at the door, indicating where Amelia was supposed to go. Her arm came down as quickly as her mouth dropped open.

"Miss Cook?" The redheaded green-eyed officer who had stepped into the room was not a stranger.

Julia closed her mouth, and nodded her head. "Good morning, Officer Allen!"

"Could I speak with you in the hall?"

Once in the hall, Officer Allen informed Julia that intruders had entered her mother's house, rendered her unconscious, and then proceeded to trash it.

Julia gasped, overcome by a feeling of guilt. Not only had she spent last night at Denny's place, both of them had turned off their cell phones. Had her mother tried to reach her?

"Mom? Someone hurt my mom?"

"She's at the hospital right now. She didn't want to go, but she didn't have a choice when the medic examined her eyes and saw unequal pupils."

Julia threw up her hands. "And they trashed her house? Whatever for?"

"That we don't know," replied Officer Allen.

"But that's all? She's going to be all right?"

"Her injuries aren't serious, so I'm sure she'll be all right. However, she did babble a bit." The worried look on Julia's face stopped Officer Allen from adding that her mother was being observed at the hospital for a possible concussion. "Uh," he tried to find a way to put it into words. "Uh, would you perhaps know anything about a dog? If that's even what she was trying to tell me. She kept saying the words 'Strabismus' and 'dog' in the same sentence."

Julia smiled in spite of the seriousness of the situation. "My mom is a realtor at Town and Country Real Estate. Renters moved out of her listing on Green Street and left a dog locked in the house. He was in there for a couple of days before the neighbors complained about the barking."

The officer shook his head in disgust.

Julia continued. "The dog has crossed eyes, and the medical term for that is strabismus. So, yes, she does have a dog named Strabismus."

Officer Allen's mouth twitched. "I learn something new every day, but do you know anything about her dog being missing?"

Julia took a deep breath. "You are going to find this hard to believe, Officer Allen, but even though I haven't talked to Mom today, I do know where the dog is."

"Really?" Officer Allen had a skeptical look on his face. "Your mother didn't tell you that her dog was missing yet you know where it is?"

Julia nodded. "If you'll wait here a minute, I'll show him to you."

Julia stepped back into the classroom and motioned Amelia to come with her. "And bring the case, please."

Amelia's face turned white. She tried to stand, but her legs wouldn't support her. Through the open door, the officer was watching Amelia's struggle.

"Something wrong with her?"

"Her name is Amelia, and she's frightened," Julia said quietly.

"What would she have to be frightened of?"

"Because Mom's missing dog is in the case that's next to her desk. I just discovered it seconds before you walked into my class."

Officer Allen's red eyebrows danced. "She has your mother's dog?"

Julia walked down the aisle and stopped at Amelia's desk.

"I promise you, there is nothing to be frightened about, Amelia. The dog you have in your case has been missing, and we just want to know how you came to have it."

She raised frightened eyes. "You promise I won't be in trouble?"

"Amelia, just pick up the case and meet us in the hall. Trust me."

Amelia sighed, picked up the case and walked out of the classroom with her head down.

When the box was opened, Officer Allen inhaled sharply and blinked his eyes several times.

Julia grinned. "Sorry, Officer Allen. I should have warned you."

He tore his eyes away from the strange-looking dog and turned his attention to the girl. Amelia looked as if she were trying to shrink into herself.

"Your name is Amelia?"

She nodded.

"What's your last name, Amelia?"

"Slagle."

Officer Allen's eyes widened. "Your dad is Judd Slagle?"

She nodded again.

"Would you tell us, please, how you came to be in possession of the dog?"

"Someone brought him to my father last night."

"Who brought him?"

"I never see the men who come to visit my father. My bedroom is right above where they meet. I can hear them through the hot-air vent in the floor."

"Did you hear anyone say why they wanted this particular dog? Seems Mrs. Cook had the dog out last night to do his business, and someone snatched the dog and drove off with him."

"They wanted the collar."

"The dog's collar?"

The officer heard Julia gasp.

"Something to tell us, Miss Cook?"

Julia, her eyes wide, exclaimed, "I…I changed the collar!"

"You changed it?"

"Yes, I did! Amelia, are you positive all they wanted from the dog was the collar?"

The girl shrugged. "All I know is what I heard. As soon as my father found out the dog didn't have the right collar, he kicked him really hard. I heard the dog yelp right before I heard the door open and slam shut."

Julia was visibly shaken. "Oh, my! I never thought my changing the collar was a big thing, but it obviously was!"

Officer Allen was intently watching her face when he asked, "Miss Cook, may I inquire why you changed it?"

Julia threw up her hands. "Because Strabismus didn't like it! When Mom rescued the dog, he had a heavy ornate collar around his neck. He kept scratching at it, so yesterday I went home for lunch and stopped at the pet store. I bought a smaller collar, and when I got home, I took the heavy one off and replaced it." She looked down at Amelia. "What was so special about the original collar?"

The girl shrugged. "I don't know because they didn't talk about it. I just know that they didn't need the dog anymore."

"But you did?" asked the officer.

"I felt bad for him, so I snuck out, got him, and hid him in my room."

"Miss Cook, where did you put the collar that you took off the dog? That's probably what the intruders were trying to find in your mother's house."

"I don't really know! I looked for it after I'd made the switch, but it wasn't anywhere that I could see. Anyhow, my lunch hour was almost up and I had to rush back to my class. After that, I guess I just forgot about it."

"Maybe they found it. If they did, you'll never hear from them again. As for the dog, it sounds like he was a throwaway, just a vehicle to transfer the collar. I can't begin to guess why."

Amelia had a worried look on her face. "What will happen to the dog? I really can't take him back home with me. I tried to leave him alone this morning but he wouldn't quit barking."

"Amelia, my mom has fallen in love with the dog so she'll want him back. Let's keep Strabismus in my classroom for the rest of the day. Would that be all right with you?"

Amelia managed a smile.

After Amelia went back to her seat, Julia turned to Officer Allen. "Should I get someone to take over my classes and go be with my mother? Do you think she needs me?"

"Your mother is upset, and rightfully so. The intruders assaulted her and violated her sense of safety within her own home. You can go to the hospital if you wish, but when I left, she was quite satisfied to have Denny McCain's company. I understand that you and Denny are friends?"

Just hearing Denny's name made Julia grin.

"Well, if Mom's okay with Denny's company, I might as well stay here. Anyway, finding a sub at this late hour would be almost impossible. I'll call the hospital and let her know that I will be bringing Strabismus home with me and I'll tell her about the collar, too."

Before Officer Allen left, he shook Julia's hand. "Now that we know what the intruders were looking for, I'll have my men check the house again. Good day, Miss Cook."

CHAPTER 9

The mystery man in the hospital room at the end of the hall fumbled around the bunched-up sheets on his bed trying to find the call button. His tongue was stuck to the roof of his mouth. Water. He needed water. Slowly, he became conscious of where he was and why. He knew that his mouth was dry because of the sedatives they gave him before every procedure.

He had lost track of the number of times he'd gone under the knife. Each trip to the operating room required weeks of recovery, and then it would happen all over again. Repairing a face and a body that had been shattered by a brutal beating took time.

Muffled footsteps slowed down as they reached his room. The blonde-haired nurse who entered his room bearing a pitcher of water with ice chips in it looked like an angel to him.

Smiling at the patient with the bandaged head, she said, "I was waiting for you to wake up."

The man nodded, and then wished he hadn't.

"There, there," she patted his shoulder. "No need to answer me. I'm going to lift your head...."

The smile on her face was replaced with a frown when her hand touched his burning skin. While taking his temperature, her eyes widened with each increase in degree. Without saying a word, she eased his head back onto the pillow, took the thermometer from his mouth, and rushed out of the room. The man could do nothing but stare longingly at the pitcher of water. The ice chips glistened and condensation was dripping down the outside.

Within minutes, he found himself on a stretcher surrounded by a white-coated team to rush him to the operating room. He tried to reach out towards the water, but his arms were heavy. It was somewhere between his room and the elevator that he lost consciousness.

Hours later, the nurse who was doing a routine check of the patient in the recovery room noticed that his eyelids were moving. The few medical professionals who had been chosen to care for the mysterious no-name patient had been sworn to secrecy. Among themselves, they had speculated as to the identity of the man. Had he been placed in a federal witness protection program? Was he a political figure? Was he a foreign despot who had chosen to rearrange his facial feature to escape execution? Early in the game, they had ruled out the possibility that he was in any way a famous actor. Those men usually just enhanced what they already had. This man, whose features had been smashed in a beating, would have a brand-new face. The fever that had sent the patient back into the operating room was from an infection in one of the previously repaired areas.

She was about to leave the room when she heard whimpering noises. Turning around, she saw the heavily bandaged man fighting with the tubes and lines running into and out of his body. With surprising strength, he pulled them out, curled his hands into fists, and swung his legs over the edge of the bed. Bandages muffled the words he was yelling at his imagined foe. When help arrived, the patient was restrained, tubes were reinstalled, and straps were stretched across his body to hold him securely in the bed.

As the fever raged, so did his dreams.

***

Back home again, lying on the couch with a cold pack under her head, Susan surveyed her trashed house. All this because of a dog collar? Julia's call had been brief but informative. Strabismus would be coming home with Julia at the end of the day and that was good. Susan had been surprised, and not in the least pleased, to learn that none of the officers who responded to her 911 call today knew anything about her frantic call to the police station last night. The police obviously didn't consider dognapping a serious crime.

Drawers had been dumped and contents of cupboards along with the cupboards had been smashed on the floor. Upholstered chairs and sofa cushions had been slashed, their innards scattered. Potted plants had been overturned and handfuls of dirt had been hurled at the walls.

Denny entered the room carrying a fresh cold pack he'd taken from the freezer.

"Here, Mrs. Cook. Give me your pack and I'll give you a fresh one."

Susan shivered as she took the one from under her head and handed it to him.

"I'm freezing!"

Denny went to the hall closet and returned with the huge fur-lined fur coat.

"Denny, thank you for being here with me. So much has happened….." She buried her face in the coat.

"Yeah. That homely little mutt turned into quite the home wrecker," he observed as he stepped over a pile of debris.

"I still think it's unbelievable how my stolen dog ended up in Julia's classroom! What are the chances of that happening?"

Denny shrugged. "It happened."

"I know it happened, but how did the girl get the dog in the first place?"

"Julia probably knows," Denny said. "We'll just have to wait for her to come home."

Susan looked thoughtful. "I wonder why the girl took Strabismus to school with her? Many kids have dogs, but they leave them at home when they go to school. Why didn't she?"

Not knowing the answer to her question, Denny didn't reply but he did glance at his cell phone to see what time it was. "She'll be home in an hour. Want me to run out and grab dinner?"

Susan smiled.

"Did the thought of eating greasy chicken just make you happy?" he asked.

"No, it wasn't the thought of food that tickled me, it was the way you checked the time. You kids and your cell phones," she chuckled. "Does anyone wear a watch anymore?"

"No one I know," Denny replied. "Who needs a watch?"

"Well, I'm not giving mine up! But I must say a bucket of chicken does sound good. I have the makings of a salad in the refrigerator."

"Will you be all right if I leave you alone?"

Susan tried to hide the feeling of panic that reared its ugly head. With a fake smile plastered on her face, she kept her voice steady as she waved away Denny's concern. "Of course I'll be all right! Just make sure you lock the door on your way out."

After the door closed behind Denny, Susan shuddered. Would she ever feel safe in her house again? She had been standing by the kitchen sink washing the breakfast dishes and pining about the loss of her dog when the feeling that she was not alone had raised the hairs on the back of her neck. If she had whirled around, she might have seen who it was that had struck her on the head. But she hadn't. She'd had nothing to tell the police when they answered her 911 call.

Sighing, she looked again at her trashed house. The police had said the upstairs didn't look any better. She'd take their word for it. The only bright spot in the whole mess was Strabismus. Julia was bringing him back to her.

CHAPTER 10

With Strabismus in her arms, Julia stood by her door as the students in her last class of the day filed past her. With few exceptions, the exiting pupils reached out a hand and patted the dog.

The addition of the dog to her classroom had resulted in some unusual occurrences. With her eyes closed, Julia leaned against the door. She needed a clear head to sort out her assessment of the day.

The students' reaction when they first saw the cross-eyed dog didn't surprise her; Strabismus was not a handsome dog. But she noted that after the initial shock wore off, the love radiating from the animal had a curious effect.

In one class, there was Jeff who was now in foster care because his whole family had perished in a house fire while he was at a sleepover across town. Jeff usually spent the class time with his head down on the desk. No one had been able to reach him...but Strabismus had. He'd picked Jeff out immediately, jumped up on the desk, and licked his face. With the dog in his lap, Jeff sat up and became a part of the class.

The Collar

In another period was Matt. Bullies had made Matt's life miserable, and although he was protected from them while he was in school, he was still shunned by most of his classmates. Ignoring all attempts made by other pupils to get his attention, Strabismus didn't budge from Matt's side. At the end of the period, the dog tried his best to follow the boy out the door.

When Amelia walked into the room, Strabismus greeted her like a long-lost friend. For the first time ever, Julia saw shy Amelia interacting with those around her.

Julia sighed, gave up trying to figure it out, and with the dog still in her arms, walked back into her empty classroom. She had important things to think about…such as the dog's collar. Now that was one funny development, if you could call anything funny that had ended in violence. Should she feel guilty that because she'd changed it, her mother had been hurt? While she gathered today's test papers to take home and correct, she came to the conclusion that while she could feel terrible that her changing the collar had been bad for her mother, that didn't mean she had to feel guilty about it. There was no way she could have known that the old collar was special.

And then, up popped two big questions: where had the original collar hidden itself, and had the intruders found it?

It was time to go home and see how Denny and her mother were getting along.

"Come on, Strabismus! We're going home."

Julia grinned at the thought of how happy her mom was going to be to get her dog back.

***

The attending nurse, in a routine check on the no-name unconscious patient whose body was defying strong antibiotics, was surprised when the chuckle that escaped through his heavily bandaged face was followed by a smacking noise that sounded like a kiss....

He was feeling a little warmth from a weak sun high in the sky. The woman in his arms was smiling up at him with such love in her blue eyes that it stunned him. The fur coat they snuggled under had some story connected to it, but whatever the story was, it escaped him for the moment; it wasn't important. The woman was, so he kissed her.

"Is he waking up?" asked a doctor who had stepped into the room to check the patient's chart.

"Something's going on," replied the nurse. "Whatever it is, I think he just kissed someone!"

The doctor laughed. "Since I haven't been home in two days, I hate to admit that even my comatose patients have a better sex life than I have! Keep me posted. His fever should be going down faster than it is." Chuckling, the two continued down the hallway on their rounds.

There was no one in the room when the patient whispered, "Susan...."

***

Julia, with Strabismus in her arms, got out of her car and was heading into the house when Denny pulled into the driveway and parked behind her. After retrieving something from the passenger seat, he hurried after Julia.

"Hey, beauty with the beast, wait up!"

"Is that the best you can come up with?" Julia laughed.

Denny looked hurt. "I thought it was quite clever."

"Is that chicken I smell?" Julia asked as he caught up with her.

"Sure is!" grinned Denny. "And you're home just in time to make the salad."

"Tell me," Julia looked into Denny's laughing eyes. "If I hadn't come home, who was going to make the salad?"

Denny shrugged.

Julia gave him a friendly shove. "I thought so."

Strabismus was straining to get out of Julia's arms and into Denny's. The tantalizing smell of the chicken reminded him that no one had thought to feed him.

"Come on, we're all hungry," Denny exclaimed. "How about if we both make the salad?"

"First, let's get this dog back with Mom. How is she?"

"She's putting up a brave front, but I know she's anxious over what happened. I need to warn you before you go in. The house is a wreck."

"Is it a mess we can clean up ourselves?"

Denny shook his head. "You'll need a professional clean-up crew to do the job. There's very little in the way of furniture that can be saved."

"That bad? Over a little collar? My God, Denny! What's so special about that collar?"

Before he could answer, Susan had flung open the door.

"Strabismus, you're home!" she cried.

"Uh, Mom, I'm your daughter, remember? I'm home, too."

"Oh, Julia, don't be touchy! You weren't lost."

Julia, pretending to pout, exclaimed, "Well, thanks a lot, Mother!"

"Don't just stand there, give him to me!" Susan ordered. Once she had him cradled in her arms, tears ran down her cheeks. "I'll bet you'd have scared off the bad guys if you'd been here when they broke in," she whispered into the dog's ear.

By this time, Julia had stepped into the house. With horrified eyes, she looked at the destruction. "Mom, this is awful! Can you save anything? Even the carpet is torn up…it's…it's all ruined!"

CHAPTER 11

Amelia, stretched out on the floor, her ear close to the floor vent grate, was straining to hear what was going on in her father's office. What she needed was a knob to turn up the volume. It wasn't until her dad yelled at someone for being stupid that the voices grew loud enough for her to hear.

"Now, wait just a minute!"

"No, I'm not waiting a minute! You knocked the woman unconscious! How the hell could she tell you anything about the collar in that condition? You're telling me that wasn't stupid?"

The loud voices overlapped each other and Amelia couldn't understand what followed. Once again, the subject of the dog's collar was causing conflict. If anyone had said why the collar was so important, Amelia hadn't heard. What she did hear next made her catch her breath. Her dad had just said *Anna Amelia*, her mother's name. She hadn't been aware that she'd cried out, but she must have, because the door to her room flew open. Her father, his face a furious mask, stood in the doorway.

"You little sneak!" he yelled.

Amelia was lying on the floor curled up in a fetal position when the first kick landed.

Later, alone in her room, she allowed herself one last sob. Crying never did any good; there was no one to hear her laugh, and there was no one to hear her cry.

The doorbell's ring roused her from her misery. Running to the window, she could see a uniformed cop standing outside the front door. Through the grate, she could hear her father swearing at the men who were still with him, urging them to run out the back door and hide in the woods behind the house.

The policeman was getting aggressive in his doorbell ringing by the time Judd Slagle opened the door and cheerfully welcomed the officer into the house.

When the officer presented his daughter's story, the air went out of Judd's lungs. The little shit had found the dog and taken him to school. Trying to keep panic from his face, he took a deep breath, and with a wave of his hand and a derisive chuckle, he dismissed her. She needed a mother, he told the cop, and while he tried his very best, sometimes his best was not enough; she told stories.

Amelia grabbed a pillow and hugged it to her aching stomach. Hearing her dad lying to the police made her feel sick. She told stories? Her own father was telling lies about her. Maybe she would take Miss Cook up on her offer and talk to her. She could show her new and old bruises and cuts...no, no, she couldn't do that. Just thinking about telling on him sent waves of fear over her. He'd kill her.

Her dad never allowed her to say her mother's name, but with her own ears, she'd heard him speak of Anna Amelia and the collar in the same sentence. With a sigh of frustration, she threw the pillow across the room.

From her window, she watched as the police car backed out and drove way. Knowing that her dad wasn't finished with her, she wasn't surprised when he stormed into her room, and she wasn't surprised at what happened next.

Added to the pain from her father's fists was the ache of an empty stomach. It was way past dinnertime but there had been no dinner for her. She just hoped that when morning came, she would be able to crawl out of bed and go to school. Maybe her father would allow her to have breakfast.

***

Julia stood by the open door to her classroom waiting for the last bell to ring. Already most of the students in her first period were waiting quietly in line while a few stragglers were speed walking, trying to get to the room before the bell sounded. Way down at the end of the hall, Julia spied a girl who was having trouble walking. In her head, Julia was hoping it wasn't Amelia, but in her heart, she knew it was. Julia waited until the bell rang and the line of students disappeared into the room before she confronted Amelia.

Quietly she asked, "Did you fall again?"

Amelia nodded.

"Want to talk to me about it?"

Amelia shook her head.

"You know, Amelia, you're going to talk to someone. If you don't want it to be me, then it will be someone else."

Amelia managed to smile at her teacher. "If I had anything to tell, I'd talk to you, Miss Cook."

"If I think that you're being mistreated, it's my job to report it. If that happens, officials will visit your home and have a talk with your dad."

Alarm flashed across the girl's face. "What would they talk to him about?"

"Oh, they'd ask him questions about how the two of you get along, and why you seem to have a different injury every week."

Amelia faked a nonchalant shrug. "I'm clumsy! So, please don't bother my dad. He wouldn't appreciate it."

"Talk to me," Julia pleaded.

The girl turned, opened her mouth, and then closed it. Finally, she said, "I will tell you something, Miss Cook."

"Yes?"

"A policeman came to the house last night."

"And?"

Amelia dropped her head. "Dad told him that I tell stories."

"About what?"

"He told them that I made up the story about the cross-eyed dog and the collar. He said that I just wanted a dog because I was lonely, even though he always tried to be a good parent."

"Is he a good parent?" asked Julia.

The girl snorted.

"Does that mean no, he isn't?"

Amelia thought hard before she nodded her head.

"So, he's not a good dad. Is that right?"

Amelia nodded.

Julia pushed forward with her questioning.

"Does he ever hurt you?"

All expression left Amelia's face. She raised her head, looked into her teacher's kind eyes, and limped into the room.

She had no doubt that Judd Slagle was abusing his daughter. Was he also part of the crew that attacked her mother and trashed her house? There were so many questions she needed to ask Officer Allen. When the officer visited Judd Slagle last night and heard his story, did the cop believe him and not Amelia? And did the police still think that what happened to Susan was just a coincidence and had no connection to the dog and his collar?

And then there was the problem of Amelia. How could she protect her if the girl wouldn't confide in her?

There were no more stragglers; the hall was empty. Julia closed the door and walked to the front of the room. She smiled as her eyes went from row to row of her now orderly and quiet students. They smiled back.

She hadn't picked the wrong profession after all.

***

Principal Sheldon looked up to see Julia Cook standing in the doorway of her office.

"You want to see me?" she called from behind her desk.

Julia nodded. "I need to talk to you about Amelia Slagle."

"Amelia? That's Judd Slagle's girl."

"You know him?"

"Not really. I just know stories about him."

"Good stories?"

"No, not good ones. He's probably the closest thing to a crime boss that we have in our little town. I hear he's quite ruthless."

"I think he's mistreating Amelia."

"You think?" Mrs. Sheldon sounded alarmed. "Did Amelia tell you that her dad was hurting her?"

"No," Julia shook her head. "She claims she's just awkward and clumsy."

Mrs. Sheldon's face contorted. "This could be trouble."

"Trouble? In what way?"

"First, are you absolutely sure Amelia is being abused?"

Julia snorted. "If she isn't being abused, then she's the most accident-prone kid in the county."

There was a wistful sound in the principal's voice when she asked, "Could there be someone else responsible for her injuries?"

Julia looked puzzled. "Mrs. Sheldon, it sounds as if you're scared of Judd Slagle."

Mrs. Sheldon nodded. "I'd be crazy not to be scared of him."

"You don't want to report my suspicions because you're scared of him? It's the law, Mrs. Sheldon, we *have* to do this!"

Mrs. Sheldon sighed. "Yes, you're right, but we also have to be sure that we do no harm. We need proof, even though she'll deny it. For her safety, we can't approach him until we make sure we have a safe place for Amelia." She paused, and then added, "You weren't here when it happened, but I suppose you know about the pending lawsuit?"

Julia had heard the story. After his teacher had reported her suspicions, an abused boy who never would admit what his father was doing to him, never came back to school. The story was that he'd been shipped out of the state to live with a relative. His father filed suit against the school system for defamation of his name and character. The case was still pending, and the court costs alone were eating into the school's meager budget.

"So what are you asking me to do? Close my eyes and pretend it isn't happening because you're afraid of a lawsuit? I can't do that!"

"No, of course you can't! What I have to do is get her into protective custody *before* her dad is approached."

"Wow!" Julia exclaimed. "Judd Slagle must be awful!"

"He is! So let's make sure we can protect Amelia without causing harm to anyone …except Judd Slagle."

Chapter 12

The white-haired patient in the isolated room at the end of the hall was sitting in a chair holding a mirror in his hand when the nurse stuck her head into his room.

"Are we feeling better today?" she asked with a smile in her voice.

The patient actually grinned at her. "We? I don't know about you, but I'm feeling pretty good."

"Oh, you know what I mean!" She waved her hand. "It's just nurse chatter."

He held up the mirror and peered into it. "What do you think of my new face?"

"Hmmm," the nurse murmured as she stepped closer to get a better look at the newly unwrapped features. "I don't know what you looked like before your accident, but I can tell you that now you are quite handsome...but...."

He lowered the mirror and looked into her eyes. "Come on, now. What's with the hesitation? Something wrong?"

"It's your hair."

"My hair? What's wrong with my hair?"

"Your new face looks much too young for a fellow who has white hair."

He raised the mirror and looked at himself. "I see what you mean. Think I should dye it? How about red? I've always liked people with red hair."

"You're joking now!" she laughed.

"No, I'm not! If you ladies can change the color of your hair anytime you want, why can't I?"

"Well, I don't think you'd look very good with red hair. But you do need some color put into that white stuff on top of your head. What color was it before it turned?"

The patient paused before he answered. Remembering the trauma of the beating that had turned his hair white overnight, he struggled to suppress a shudder.

"Brown. Just ordinary brown."

"Boring brown, eh? How about becoming a blond? Want to have more fun?"

Looking at himself in the mirror, he remembered when he had been a blond. "No, been there, done that."

The nurse raised her eyebrows. "You did that? At one time in your life, you bleached your hair blond? Really?"

The man nodded. "I think I'll just leave my white hair alone. It kinda goes with my limp."

"I know you've had a lot of therapy."

"It's my own fault that I limp," he paused, wondering why he was even considering letting the nurse have a peek into his private life. *Oh, what the hell,* he thought. *I'm tired of being just the mystery man.*

"As soon as the doctors assured me that I wasn't going to die, I left the hospital and the physical therapists. There was someone I had to check on."

"Ah," the nurse smiled. "A woman?"

The man's features softened. Even talking to someone about the woman made him smile.

"Yes," he grinned. "A woman."

"Did it make her happy to know you were checking on her?"

His face shut down and the smile left his face. He was remembering sneaking into Susan's house for one last glimpse of her before going back to the hospital. Unfortunately, she hadn't been asleep; he still had regrets about scaring her. A terrified Susan had almost seen him before he made his escape.

The nurse backed away. She knew that the door to his private life had just been slammed shut.

Acting as if the last bit of conversation had never happened, he continued, "Eventually the therapists began to come to my house to work with me. They did a good job and I was able to walk by the time I was ready to return to the hospital to rebuild my face. But by delaying the start of therapy, I'm afraid that I'll be limping for the rest of my life. So the white hair stays."

The nurse didn't push. The man had been here for months, and this was the first time he had let anyone get a glimpse of who he was.

"You've been here a long time," the nurse remarked. "Will you be leaving us anytime soon?"

"I can leave anytime," the man replied. And then, with a faraway look in his eyes, he added, "I just don't know if I want to."

The nurse had her mouth open to ask another question when she heard her name being paged. He was relieved to see her rush out of the room.

The answer he'd given the nurse had surprised him. Finally, he had put his feelings into words.

***

Susan paced from wall to wall in the small cramped motel room her homeowner's insurance agent had rented for her while her ransacked house was being restored. From his nest on the unmade bed, Strabismus' eyes followed her. Every once in a while he'd wave his tail back and forth, trying to figure out when it was time for him to join whatever game she was playing.

She had found out the hard way why Julia's student had taken the dog to school with her that day. Strabismus didn't like to be left out of anything or, heaven forbid, left behind. On the one day she'd actually gone to work and left Strabismus behind in the motel room, it had taken just forty-five minutes before the manager called Susan threatening to kick her and the dog out if something wasn't done about the noise Strabismus was making. The incident sent Susan to the pet store to buy a dog-carrier.

She was visibly agitated, and it wasn't her trashed house or her new dog that was causing her anxiety. If someone had asked what was making her feel so uneasy, it would have been hard for her to put her feelings into words. She just knew she should not be away from her house and stuck here in the motel.

The phone rang.

Jarred out of her pensive mood, she grabbed the phone and yelled, "What?"

Julia was laughing. "Mother, haven't I taught you better manners? That's no way to answer the phone!"

"Oh, it's you," Susan answered in a flat voice.

"Yes, it's me. You were expecting someone else?"

"Ah, no…not really. What's up?"

"Denny has invited me to stay with him instead of with you at the motel."

Susan didn't say anything.

"Mother? Are you there?"

"Of course I'm here! Staying with Denny is okay with me. This room is really too small for both of us anyhow."

"You sound strange, Mom. Are you sure about this?"

"Sure? Of course I'm sure! I just hope the work at the house doesn't take long."

"Don't count on that, Mom. After all, the carpeting and most of the furniture has to be replaced, pictures reframed…."

Susan broke into Julia's recitation of things to be done. "I know, Julia, you don't have to remind me."

"Do you have plans for today? Are you going to the office?"

"Quit worrying about me!" Susan spoke harshly. "I have my own plans."

"You do? What are they?"

"Just go, Julia! I'm busy."

Susan hung up the phone, grabbed Strabismus, and headed for the car. She didn't question why, but she was in a hurry to go home. The urge to sit on her front porch wrapped in *his* fur coat was overwhelming.

CHAPTER 13

Judd Slagle had been sure he'd broken his wife's spirit. After all, she no longer defied his orders, and after years of physical abuse, she was finally behaving as a good wife should. He was shocked when she died suddenly.

It was days after her funeral when he was going through her possessions that he found a small notebook with puzzling entries. At first, nothing made sense until he picked up the last book she'd been reading before she died, and a packet of bank deposit slips and a rental slip for a safety deposit box dropped out.

He hadn't broken his wife after all.

***

There is something therapeutic about staring death in the face. Up until the doctor had spoken the words "You have inoperable cancer", the most troubling thing in Anna Amelia's life had been her miserable marriage. Her wealthy parents had intensely disliked the man she had chosen to marry. Insisting that they were wrong, Anna went against their wishes and married the handsome Judd Slagle. At first glance, Judd was an exceptionally good-looking man. Tall, fit, and with hair that was

72

prematurely turning white, he looked like every woman's dream. Only his cold eyes gave away the secret. It didn't take many months of marriage for her to admit that her parents had been right. Judd was a "hands-on" type of man. His first reaction to any situations was a good slap, a well-placed punch, or a twisted arm.

Anna, who had fought so hard against her parents' wishes, was too embarrassed to admit they had been right. Not only had she painted a picture of her marriage in loving colors, she had also presented them with their first grandchild.

Feeling guilty about their initial attempts to keep Anna out of what was obviously a wonderful union, her parents assuaged these feelings by giving her gifts. At first, she had insisted that their apology had been enough. The doctor issuing the death sentence changed her mind.

Something had to be done about Amelia. There never had been any indication that Judd viewed his daughter as anything other than an annoyance. What would happen to Amelia when her mother was no longer around to keep her out of Judd's way? Anna always paid a high price for protecting her daughter.

On the morning of the telephone call, Anna had been sitting at the breakfast table staring into a cup of cold coffee, pondering her next move. Trying to hide her parents' gifts was becoming a problem. She knew it was just a matter of time before Judd stumbled onto her stash. It wasn't as if she could go to the phone and call a friend for help; she had no friends. Friends would insist on knowing why she limped or why her legs were black and blue. It was just easier not having questioning eyes around her. Judd had already left the house and Amelia was still in bed when the jarring noise of the telephone interrupted her thoughts.

"Hello?"

"Hello?" answered a faint voice.

"Hello?" Anna tried again.

"Anna Amelia, is that you?"

"Yes. And you are?" Anna could hear heavy breathing.

"Honey," the caller paused to cough. "I'm Judd's mother."

Anna snorted. Early in their relationship, she'd cried when Judd described how he had thrown caution to the wind, placed himself in great danger while trying to save his mother from a burning house. With his head bent and tears running down his cheeks, he confessed to Anna that he'd failed; his mother had died despite his efforts. Anna had been so moved she'd gathered him into her arms and rocked him like a baby.

"Are you still there?"

"What kind of a call is this?"

The caller's chuckle ended with a coughing spasm.

"He told you that his mother was dead, didn't he, honey? But wishing me dead doesn't make me dead."

"B...but," stammered Anna.

"I need to see you."

"See you? Where are you?"

"I'm quite close. I've always been close."

Quite close? Anna looked frantically around her kitchen. Was someone pulling a not-so-funny joke on her?

"I don't think...no, you can't be Judd's mother. I'm hanging up."

Anna hadn't made it back to her cold coffee before the phone rang. It was only the fear that Judd might be calling her that made her pick up the receiver.

"My son has a scar on the inside of his left arm from running into a barbed wire fence when he was eight years old. There's a mole on his body that only a mother and a wife should know about. He has...."

"It's you again!" Anna complained. "This is not funny."

"It never was funny, Anna. Please listen to me because what I have to tell you is important."

"You're still insisting that you're his mother?"

With a laugh that was cut short by a cough, she replied, "Why would I claim to be the mother of a monster if I weren't? Believe me, I take no pride in being his mother."

Anna's legs were shaking.

"Now, will you listen to me?" the woman asked.

Anna reached out and pulled a kitchen chair close to the phone. "I think I'd better sit down."

"If anyone could understand why I've been hiding all these years, it's you, Anna."

With a catch in her voice, she asked, "H...he hurt you?"

"Are you surprised?"

Anna sighed. "All right, I'll listen. Please, why are you calling?"

"I'm a sick woman, Anna, and I need to give you some things before...before," she paused. "Ah, hell, I'll just come right out and say it. Before I die."

"You're going to die?"

As if to prove a point, the woman coughed. When she finally caught her breath, she continued.

"I know Amelia will be leaving to catch the bus in an hour."

"You know her schedule?"

The woman chuckled. "Of course I know her schedule! I've been watching my granddaughter for years."

Anna gasped.

"Come on, Anna! I'm not a stalker! I'm just a lonely grandmother who has been placed in this position by an abusive son. Now, I know you're sick. Don't ask me how, but I know that both of us are living on borrowed time. As I see it, my son is not going to take care of Amelia once we're both gone. Honey, it's up to the two of us to do that. I'll say it again. I need to see you."

"You said you were close. How close?"

"I live in the apartment building across the street from Amelia's school. My unit is 4B."

"Are you…are you talking about today? I should come to see you this morning?"

"Why not? Do you have something better to do?"

Anna Amelia thought about the tedious day that she had to look forward to. Going to see Judd's mother took on the air of an adventure, something that had been missing from her life for years.

"I'll come right after Amelia's bus pulls out. By the way, what do I call you? After all, you are my mother-in-law."

"My name is Minnie. The door will be unlocked. When you get here, just walk in."

Anna stood for a long time in the middle of the kitchen floor marveling at the change one telephone call can make. She was actually excited about something.

***

Just as she had said, Minnie died. Judd, being the next of kin, had been contacted. He was surprised that she had lived so close to him. The only time he'd tried to find her was when he discovered that the family home had been sold. The house was an expensive one, and as her only child, he felt he deserved a portion of the proceeds. There was no doubt in his mind that there were things he could do to encourage her to share, but he couldn't find her. She had disappeared.

What he did find was that she had died destitute. Her will had cut him out of receiving anything, which didn't mean much because there was nothing to receive. What had happened to the money from the sale of the million-dollar family home? What about his father's extensive investment portfolio? There was no way that she could she have died penniless.

***

Cancer hadn't been the culprit that silenced Anna; it was a stroke that had taken her months before the oncologist's estimated time. A week after the funeral, Judd's world was rocked by what he found in the envelopes that had dropped out of the last book Anna had been reading. How had Anna kept the existence of the bank accounts and a deposit box from him? Since the only money he had ever given her was for groceries, what was she doing with a bank account and a deposit box?

As his eyes searched for the source of the accumulated wealth, the shock of seeing an official notarized document, signed by his mother, transferring all her assets to Anna stole the breath from his body. His own mother had used his wife to stab him in the back. Listed were the sale of his parents' house, the stocks and bonds from his father's portfolio, and the family jewels. Several entries showed the money and jewels that had come from Anna's wealthy parents. How had she kept that from him? The total amount of stocks, bonds, and jewelry in the box had to be in the millions. Where the actual cash was deposited was another matter. That information had to be in the box, too.

He had just recovered from the shock of what his own mother had done with assets that should have been his, when he unfolded a legal document and realized he was looking at a copy of his wife's will. When had she made a will? His heart was beating fast, thinking about what he would do when he got his hands on all the wealth she had left him. But weren't heirs supposed to be notified of a will when the person died? That's when he realized his name wasn't mentioned in the will. He wasn't an heir. Amelia was.

Hot, murderous rage filled him. He was sorry Anna was dead because right now he wanted to feel the joy of killing her with his bare hands. How could she do this to him?

After he calmed down, he saw that there was one more document that had been legally filed. It stated that Judd Slagle was forbidden access to the box even if, by some chance, he gained possession of the key and was in the company of a bank official.

Judd sat quietly for a long time, trying to digest what he had just uncovered. There had to be a way to get his hands on all that wealth. No way was he going to allow it to go to the daughter he had never wanted in the first place. Anna certainly hadn't had the sophisticated knowledge to put the plan together, and he was sure his mother didn't have it either. So someone from the bank had helped them. He had noticed that the name Ralph had found its way into one entry in the notebook. That was the only piece of information he had to work with.

To get into a safety deposit box, the renter is given a key, and the bank has the master key. Both keys are needed to open the box. Judd didn't have a key but he did have Ralph's name.

***

Ralph Young, a well-respected man in the small town as well as a long-time bank employee, had been the one who had helped the two women. He also was in charge of the bank's mortgage department. On the day that he had agreed to meet Judd Slagle in the secluded back booth at the Omelet Shop, the bank had foreclosed on a house on Green Street. Ralph had entered the restaurant a happy man with a lovely family, a great job, and a clear conscious. He was also a pillar in the local Presbyterian Church. His meeting with Judd changed all that. During the days that followed, he had trouble concentrating on his bank duties; at night, his dreams terrified him. All he had to do was close his eyes, and the restaurant scene replayed in his mind, over and over, and word for word....

A benign-looking Judd Slagle, whose prematurely white hair made him look like a kindly grandfather, joined Ralph in the back booth at the Omelet Shop.

Over a cup of coffee, Judd asked Ralph to do something that was repugnant to the Presbyterian elder. An indignant Ralph pushed his coffee aside and stood up. "Absolutely not," he said. That was when Judd casually mentioned what would happen to Ralph's wife and daughter if he didn't comply. He demanded a key to the bank box.

Startled, Ralph was broadsided by Judd's threat to harm his family. It hit him that the stories that the two women had told about Judd hadn't been an exaggeration.

Striving to keep his voice from shaking, he replied calmly, "I don't have a key to your box. The last time I saw the key, your wife had it."

"Well, I guess you don't really love your wife and kid," Judd said as he slid across the bench and out of the booth.

"Wait a minute!" Ralph cried. "Let me think! Both your mother and your wife are dead. You would have to show up, not only with the key, but also with proof that you are the executor of their estates. You are not the executor of anything! But there's another problem!"

Judd scoffed. "I don't want to hear about problems! It's your job to get rid of them."

"I can't get rid of a signed and witnessed restraining order that keeps you from even going near the box, let alone opening it!"

"That's all?" Judd scoffed. "You and I could pull this off without anyone knowing what box I was opening."

"What other box? You don't have a box." Ralph was sweating.

"But I will, because you're going to rent one for me."

"You'll go into the vault with me while flashing your key so everyone can see it, but I'll pull out Anna's box instead and open it with my master key," Ralph said flatly, reading Judd's plan from his face.

Judd grinned. "Now that wasn't so hard, was it?"

"I can't open it with just the master key. I need Anna's key. And then there's something else...."

Judd's face clouded when Ralph covered his face with his hands.

"What now? Another problem?"

Ralph had stalled as long as he could. He was just too terrified to come up with any more objections. Who was he kidding? There was no way he was going to get out of the restaurant without telling Judd what he wanted to know. What he was about to do now was something he thought he'd never do. He was going to break the promise he had made to this horrible man's mother and his wife.

"Spit it out, man! What other problem?"

Ralph closed his eyes and silently asked God to forgive him. In a flat voice, he stated the problem. "There's nothing in the box"

"Empty?" Judd yelled. "The box is empty?"

Heads turned their way. "Not so loud! Yes, the box is empty. Minnie and Anna emptied it before either one of them died."

Judd hissed. "You are the one who set this whole thing up. Don't even try to tell me that you didn't know what they had done!"

"No, I didn't know anything until shortly before Anna died. Your wife took Minnie's passing very hard. She knew her days were numbered, and the thought of what the two of them had done scared her. Now that Minnie was gone, she was the only one who knew where they had hidden the content of the box."

"That bitch! I'm gonna kill her!" Judd hissed.

"You're a little late for that," Ralph reminded him.

Judd's cold eyes made Ralph wish he'd kept his mouth shut.

Judd closed those cold eyes, took a deep breath, and whispered, "Please, please tell me that Anna told you where they hid the stuff."

Before he answered, Ralph looked around for the closest exit in case he might have to run for his life when Judd heard his answer.

"No, she didn't."

Lunging across the table, Judd grabbed Ralph's collar. "Don't mess with me!" he hissed.

Ralph choked. "Put me down! People are watching us!"

Judd gave one last jerk on the collar before he released Ralph who was having trouble regaining his breath.

"Judd," Ralph asked, "do you have any idea how much your own mother and wife hated you?"

Judd shrugged. "So?"

"They also didn't trust you, but they trusted me." Ralph's eyes filled with tears knowing that he was about to break that trust.

"How touching," Judd scoffed. "Get on with it!"

Ralph took a deep breath, and continued. "They'd moved everything, fearing that somehow you'd find out about the box. Anna wanted to tell me where they had stashed it, but I didn't want to know anything about it. They'd told me stories about you, and because I didn't trust myself to keep their secret, I wouldn't listen to them."

Judd's eyes were wild. "Are you saying that they hid all that wealth and now no one knows where it is?"

"Your wife gave me a sealed envelope."

"And you never opened it?"

Ralph hesitated but a moment. It was fear of Judd that had kept him from disclosing the fact that an envelope even existed. He fervently wished that he'd gotten rid of it...but he hadn't. Right now, it was inside his jacket pocket, burning a hole in his heart. No amount of trust that had been placed in him was worth losing his wife and daughter. He reached inside his jacket and pulled out an envelope with Amelia's name on it.

"Here it is. It wasn't mine to open."

Judd recognized his dead wife's handwriting. "Well, would you look at this! A message from the great beyond!"he cackled.

Grabbing the envelope, he ripped it open. The scrap of paper that fell out had one handwritten sentence.

"It says 'Look inside the dog's collar.' What dog? What collar?"

"Oh, my God!" Ralph cried. "The dog's collar?"

Judd slammed his fist down on the table, "I'll ask you again, what dog?"

Ralph was having trouble absorbing the words in the note. Finally, he asked quietly, "Did you know your mother had a dog?"

"Of course I didn't know she had a dog!" Judd growled. "I didn't even know where she was living. I had to find that out after she died."

"Quiet down! People are looking at us!" Ralph whispered hoarsely. "Well, she did have a little dog that she rescued from the pound. Nobody wanted it because it was ugly and cross-eyed. "

"Is that the dog with the collar?"

"Has to be. There's no other dog that I know of. Your mother loved the dog, and she made me agree to take him when she died."

"So the dog is living with you?"

"Yes, but I must say he's been a big bother because he barks all the time, and when he greets visitors at the door, he's so ugly and weird looking they freak out. I almost got rid of him last week."

"Does he wear a collar that something could be hidden in?"

"He does. In fact, your mother made a big fuss over the special collar that she'd had made. It's really too large for the dog, but she made me promise not to change collars. I thought it was just an old lady's whim...."

"I want the dog!" Judd demanded.

"You're welcome to the yappy dog. I'll be glad to get rid of him."

Ralph knew what he had just done went against everything he believed in. But if he hadn't done it, what Judd would do to his family...Ralph winced even thinking about the threats. He had to come up with a way to get the dog to Judd that couldn't be traced back to him.

Ralph closed his eyes and prayed for a solution. While praying, his hand found its way into a pocket...and his fingers felt a key. His eyes jerked open. Should he do this? Did he have a choice? No, he didn't have a choice. He held out the key.

"I'll lock the dog in a house that the bank owns. The squatters have been kicked out of the house at 2503 Green Street. It's going to be put on the market, so don't waste any time in picking him up. Here's the key."

A grinning Judd grabbed the key and walked out. Ralph waited a moment to leave. He didn't want to be seen with Mr. Slagle any more than he already had.

Ralph opened his eyes, and willed his memory to stop replaying the restaurant scene. And it did stop...until he closed his eyes....

CHAPTER 14

There was no love in the cold eyes of Judd Slagle as he watched his daughter's slow and obviously painful approach to the bus stop. With a shaky hand, he smoothed down his wind-blown white hair. Maybe he'd used his fists too enthusiastic last night. The last thing he needed was some goody-goody teacher reporting him for child abuse.

He could see the bus turning into their street and, as usual, Amelia had it timed so that she would be the last one to board the bus. Even though he knew why she did this every morning, it never occurred to him that he should feel guilty. In his mind, the one who should feel guilty was his dead wife. How dare she leave him nothing but a daughter to raise who he'd never wanted in the first place.

And now, that unwanted daughter was causing him trouble. He had no way of knowing how much the police knew. The picture in his mind of what he had seen when he'd flung open her bedroom door was as upsetting now as it had been last night. How long and how often had the little sneak listened through the register? And who had she told?

He and his men hadn't found the collar in the house they'd trashed. Kidnapping the woman and making her talk was probably not a good idea. If they believed any of Amelia's stories, the police might be already fingering them as the house trashers. Anger against the man whose blow to the woman's head had rendered her unconscious before he'd had a chance to quiz her rose hot again. He had to admit that there was something good about it. Since the woman hadn't seen anything, she couldn't identify anyone.

For his own sanity, he had to believe that the police viewed the whole thing as nothing more than his daughter's wild story.

***

Across town, another white-haired man looked at himself in the three-way mirror. Starting from scratch, he was slowly building a wardrobe, but he hadn't yet decided what he wanted to be. In his former life, he'd been a professional golfer. His face and hair were different, but from the back, he still looked like Ryan Wilcox. One huge difference was his voice. A blow to his throat had changed it.

He glanced again at his image and decided to buy the run-of-the-mill outfit. It gave him a casual look, it was nothing special, and it certainly wouldn't draw attention; it would go nicely with the other similar items hanging in his motel closet.

Would Susan recognize him? Being identified as the golfer who was supposed to be dead was dangerous. He doubted if he would be lucky enough to survive another attempt on his life.

His life as a professional golfer had ended after he exposed a very lucrative scam. Athletes were being injured and sometimes killed to improve the odds of a gambling ring. Even though the top men in the ring were still in prison, that didn't stop them from punishing the one person who had caused their fall; a high-paying contract to kill Ryan had been issued.

For ten years, he had managed to stay alive by hiding. It was only his well-executed escape plans and the winnings from several lucrative tournaments stashed in offshore accounts that had kept him alive the several times they had found him. Ryan was living in a small western Michigan town that bordered the big lake when they once again picked up his trail. He had become bored with his solitary existence and talked himself into believing that nothing much could happen to him while he was out with a realtor looking at houses that he never intended to buy. As luck would have it, the realtor who answered the phone when he called to make an appointment was Susan Cook. He told her his name was Charles Holiday.

Susan Cook. Just thinking her name softened the lines on his face. But because of him, bad things had happened to Susan. Remembering what he had exposed her to made the hard lines reappear on his face.

He shook his head as if to stop the memories; it didn't work. He cringed when he remembered crashing the small plane while he and Susan were fleeing his pursuers. Susan had been unscathed, but an injury to his head had given him amnesia for a short time.

One of the pursuers was Ted, his look-alike first cousin who was also his old caddy. It was Ted who'd found him. The contract was to kill the golfer, but Ted didn't want to kill him quickly; he wanted him to suffer. It had taken years, but eventually the envy of his famous cousin had grown into an all-consuming volatile state. While Ryan danced in the charmed spotlight, no one paid any attention to his lookalike-caddy, the cousin who faded into the background. When Ted had walked away from the battered and dead body of the golfer, he felt free for the first time in years. Now he and Ryan's wife, Laura, could continue their affair in the open. They had been sneaking around under Ryan's nose, and he never suspected a thing. Life was sweet, and it would be even sweeter when he collected on the contract.

Ryan lived.

To Ryan, while the actual pain of being beaten and left for dead was severe, it wasn't as devastating as the ache of being separated from Susan. Against his doctor's orders, he'd checked himself out of the hospital as soon as it became apparent that he was going to survive, chartered a plane, and flew to Susan's hometown. He had moved into the house across the street from her. Mornings when the attendant rolled his wheelchair out on the porch, his eyes would search for her, and there she'd be, sitting on the swing. It was almost as if she were waiting for him. But how could she know? Wrapped in his fur coat, she would wait until the attendant left him, and then she'd wave to him.

The coat had been a joke-gift from a fellow golfer. He'd complained so loudly and bitterly over playing a spring tournament game during a snowstorm that the coat had been presented to him at the awards banquet. He'd worn the huge coat while he made an acceptance speech that had them all laughing. If the expensive coat was just a prop for a funny joke, then the joke was on them because he hadn't given it back.

One morning his heart threatened to stop beating when Susan had actually left her porch and started walking toward him. For some reason, she stopped in the middle of the street, changed her mind, and went back to her seat on the porch.

Oh, how he longed to see her, to hold her and never let her go, but that was not the time for her to see him. He had waited until the therapists had him on his feet before he moved out of the house one night and returned to the hospital to rebuild his face.

It had taken many surgeries and months of rehab to get him to where he was today. Glancing at himself in the mirror, he narrowed his eyes and asked the reflection, "Who are you?"

"Are you talking to me?" questioned the clerk who had been helping him pick out the outfit.

Flustered, he chuckled. "No, I was talking to myself. But I'll ask you a question. What profession do you think I'm in?"

The clerk thought for a moment. "You look intelligent, successful, and, by the way, quite handsome. You are...you are...yes! You are an investment banker!"

Why not? Ryan thought. "Is it that obvious?" he laughed. "I'm taking the outfit, and thank you for your assistance. You've been very helpful."

Leaving the store, he walked to his car, opened the door, and hung his new outfit inside. In deep thought, he stood by the open door to the driver's side, jiggling his keys. Dare he? Was it too soon?

Once the decision was made, Ryan crawled into the car, started it, and spun the tires as he headed for Susan's street. How much trouble could he get into just by driving past her house?

Driving slowly through the neighborhood where he had lived, he was pleased to notice that the houses and lawns were well cared for. He was really seeing things for the first time. A hospital ambulance had brought him here, and when he left to go back to the hospital, it had been in the middle of a dark night. He had no idea if the house he was looking for was in the middle or the end of the block. All he knew was that he would recognize Susan's house no matter where it was because he'd lived across the street and stared at it for weeks.

He noticed that straight ahead was a house with multiple trucks and cars parked on the street. He watched as a steady stream of workers hauled lamps, smashed picture frames, and broken chairs from the house to a truck that was parked in the driveway. When he got abreast of it, he saw that it was Susan's house. His heart skipped a beat. At that moment, the front door opened and Susan, carrying his coat and a case, stepped out and sat down on the swing.

Ryan struggled to regain control of his emotions. He had never believed in love at first sight, and really, it hadn't been at first sight. It had happened in the time that seemed compressed in the few days that he had spent with her. Finding Susan was like finding his other half. He wouldn't have thought such a thing possible had it not happened to him. But it had; he desperately needed that other half. Susan thought he was dead. Had she moved on? Black dread filled his heart. What if she had found someone else in the time he had spent recovering from Ted's beating? Then, as he thought about what he had just seen, the black dread fled.

She was wrapped up in *his* coat.

CHAPTER 15

Wrapped in the coat, Susan and Strabismus sat on the porch swing and watched the cars drive past her house. The anxious feeling that she had struggled with as she had driven home was gone. Even the noise created by those who were putting her house back together didn't bother her. She was content.

The workers hadn't made her feel welcome when she walked into her own house. Two men carrying out the damaged sofa had bumped into her, and when she scurried to get out of their way, she'd backed into the project manager who was bringing coffee for his crew. Mumbling apologies, she hurried into the kitchen where she stumbled into a worker who was looking anxiously at his commercial vacuum that was making death-rattling sounds. The kitchen had been torn apart, and to make vacuuming easier, the stove had been pulled away from the wall.

"Your machine doesn't sound too healthy," Susan yelled over the noisy machine.

The worker nodded. "It can handle pretty big chunks, but this time I think it bit off more than it can chew," he yelled back.

Whatever it had been that was choking the vacuum finally got through. Susan nodded to the man and continued out the door to the swing.

Later that day, the full bag that contained the much sought after dog collar was taken off the commercial vacuum and thrown into the truck along with the rest of the debris slated to be taken to the dump.

***

As Ryan drove back to his motel room, his thoughts were of Susan and not on driving. When the old clunker of a car ahead of him slowed down to a crawl before it gave one last sigh and stopped altogether, he almost plowed into the back of it.

The door of the old car opened and a tall, friendly-looking young man crawled out. Ryan could have driven around and continued his journey back to the motel, but he didn't. He pulled to the side of the road and parked.

The young man approached Ryan as he was getting out of his car.

"Hey, thanks, man!" he exclaimed as he stuck out his hand.

Ryan laughed as he shook it. "Why are you thanking me? I haven't done anything yet."

"I was thanking you for not running into the back of me! The old lady really died this time."

Ryan looked at the stalled car. "I used to own a similar car years ago. I learned to take it apart and put it back together again. Do you mind if I look at it?"

"Be my guest," grinned the young man. "By the way, my name is Denny."

For a second, Ryan panicked. Inventing new names for himself was getting old. Would the time ever come when he wouldn't have to hide his identity? He needed to remember the name that was on several bogus documents in his pocket....

"K...Keith. My name is Keith. Nice to meet you, Denny."

"Well Keith, could you help me push the car off the road?" Denny asked.

"You steer and I'll push," was the reply.

Later, with both their heads under the hood, Denny exclaimed, "There! That's the problem!" Reaching for the troubling engine part, he accidentally shoved Ryan's hand into a puddle of standing oil.

"Oh, Jeez man! I'm sorry!" Denny fussed.

Ryan didn't know whether to laugh or to cry as he held up his black hand.

"If you're looking for a rag to clean your hand, I'm afraid I don't have one. But I think my car's fixed!"

Ryan waved his hand. "Any suggestions?" he asked.

"Tell you what," Denny exclaimed. "My girlfriend lives in this neighborhood. If you don't mind riding with me, I'll take you there and get you cleaned up. It's the least I can do for someone who stopped to help me."

Ryan hesitated. He did have on one of his new outfits and knowing how hard an oil stain is to remove, he agreed. "Think it's okay to leave my car here?"

"In this neighborhood?" Denny laughed. "You don't even have to lock it." He paused and the smile left his face. Could he say the neighborhood was safe, considering what had happened to Susan's house?

Ryan crawled into the old clunker that now started at the first try.

"Looks like you fixed it," he said to Denny.

"I'm getting better at it," Denny replied. "My dad, when he was around, used to keep it running."

"He's not around anymore?" Ryan asked.

Denny was silent. At last, he said, "No, he's not."

By that time, they were pulling up to the house that had all the trucks and cars parked around it. Ryan's heart almost stopped.

"Having second thoughts?" Denny asked as he came around and opened Ryan's door.

"No, I just didn't want to touch the handle with my dirty hand," he managed to say as he crawled out.

Denny pointed to the house. "You're going to meet Susan, my future mother-in-law," he grinned. "At least that's what I'm planning."

Ryan was having trouble breathing. "Why all the cars and trucks?" *Please don't say she's moving,* he mentally pleaded with Denny.

"Those belong to the workers who are fixing her trashed house."

"Her house got trashed?"

"Yeah, sure did!"

"Do you know who did it?"

"Intruders."

Ryan stopped walking.

Denny grinned. "Oh, you worried about your unlocked car? Believe me, this neighborhood is safe…" Denny paused while they watched a workman carry a smashed chair out of the house. "Well, it usually is."

94

"Ah, did the intruders hurt anyone?" Ryan asked the question and then held his breath as he waited for the answer.

"They knocked Susan out and trashed the house. There's very little that they didn't wreck."

"Knocked her out?" Ryan reached out and grabbed Denny's arm. "Is she okay?"

Puzzled by his reaction, Denny looked down at the hand that was gripping his arm to make sure it wasn't the oily one. "She spent a few hours at the hospital, but yeah, she's okay."

By that time, they'd arrived in front of the house. Susan, wrapped in his coat and holding some strange looking animal, was watching them.

Ryan's body went rigid. He wasn't ready for this.

"Denny, I've changed my mind. It was nice meeting you," he managed to mumble. With his mouth so dry, it was hard to move his tongue.

Denny's smile was replaced with a frown as he watched the stranger turn around, and in a labored trot, head back towards his car.

Susan stood up, and the coat and Strabismus fell to the floor. "Who was that man?" she asked.

"A really nice guy! I don't know what happened to make him leave like that. My car stalled, and he got dirty helping me fix it. I was bringing him back here because his one hand was covered with oil."

"I don't know how I should feel about this," she mused. "He took one look at me and ran. Was he limping?"

"Limping? I think maybe he was, but I'm sure his running away had nothing to do with you, Susan. Any man would be proud and lucky to meet you."

"So says my hopeful future son-in-law. Do you think your opinion might just be a bit slanted?"

"Ah, go on, Susan! Your daughter is beautiful and so are you."

Susan turned around, picked up her coat and the dog, and stepped off the porch.

"Since I'm just getting in the way of the workers, I'm going back to the motel. What are you and Julia doing for dinner?"

"Didn't Julia tell you that it's Parent-Teacher Night at her school? She's not coming home until it's over. It could be a long night. Some of the parents work late and she has to stay for them."

Susan couldn't get the image of the strange man out of her head. She had seen the many expressions that flashed across his face right before he turned and limped away. Something about the whole thing was making her restless. Going back to the motel to spend the night alone wasn't something she wanted to do.

"Denny, may I buy you dinner? I don't want to eat alone tonight."

He put his hands in his pocket and looked at the ground. "You don't have to buy me dinner."

Susan poked him in the ribs. "Come on. I know you're a new real estate salesman who won't get a check until he makes a sale."

Denny looked wistful. "Do you think that's ever going to happen?"

Susan shrugged. Working on commissions is always an iffy business.

CHAPTER 16

Ryan was breathing hard and his leg was objecting by the time he got to his car. He opened the door, sat down, and leaned his head on the steering wheel. What a pathetic, gutless, cowardly, weak, useless, spineless chicken! He could have come up with even more names if he hadn't burst into tears.

He never saw the car that slowed down as it passed him.

Denny, in the passenger seat of Susan's car, saw him first.

"Hey, that's him."

"Who?"

"The guy who ran off because you're so ugly," teased Denny.

"What was he doing?"

"He was either laughing or crying."

"What makes you say that?"

"Well, he had his hands over his face and his shoulders were shaking."

"He could be ill and that's why he ran off. Should I turn around and go back? Maybe he needs help."

Denny thought, and then shook his head. "No man wants a pretty woman to see him crying, if that's what he was doing."

"So now I'm pretty?"

"Yes, you're pretty and I'm pretty hungry. Let's just leave the man alone."

Susan started to laugh. "Denny, didn't you say he had oil on one of his hands?"

"Yeah, so what?"

"If he had his hands over his face, don't you wonder what his face looks like now?"

"Oh, oh," Denny grinned. "That just proves the theory that no good deed goes unpunished. I'm sure he'll figure out that he has oil on his face all by himself. Let's eat."

Susan made a face. "You're all heart! Where are we going? Any restaurant in mind?"

Strabismus, who had been asleep in the back seat, woke up and let loose with a few musical notes.

"What about your dog?"

"What about him?"

Strabismus sang.

"You can't take him into a restaurant, and if you leave him in the car, he'll howl the whole time we're in there."

Susan had a pained look on her face. "You're right. I haven't gone anywhere but work since I've had him, and for that I just put him in his cage and carry him with me. Well, how about a fast-food-drive-through?"

The dog thought that was worthy of only three notes.

The Collar

Since Susan was buying, Denny had been hoping for something better than a drive-through. His disappointment disappeared when he remembered a fast-food ad.

"Susan, how does an Angry Burger sound to you? It has jalapeño peppers, bacon...."

***

After heaving one last sob, Ryan wiped his tear-stained face on his jacket sleeve. He couldn't remember if he'd ever before in his life cried that hard. It had been the thought of seeing her again that had given him the will to live. During the months of operations and therapies, the memory of her and the need to be with her was stronger than the pain from the procedures. He had just had his big chance for a casual meeting with her, and he'd blown it. Meeting her now was going to seem planned and artificial.

Finding his key, he started the car and glanced into his mirror to see if he'd wiped off all traces of his crying. To his surprise, he viewed his oil-smeared face, and then to his horror, he saw his oil-smeared jacket sleeve. Serves me right, he thought. He had been planning to eat dinner at a nice restaurant, but since he had nothing to clean his face and hand, it was with regret that he pulled into the parking lot of a fast-food drive-through.

There was a short line of cars waiting their turn to speak into the order box. The car ahead of him was abreast of the box when Ryan became aware of a dog in the car. As he watched, it crawled up the back of the seat and looked at him through the back window. The sight of a strange-looking cross-eyed dog staring at him wiped the sadness from his eyes and put a smile on his face. He was still smiling when the driver of the car reached out her open window to accept the food.

It was Susan.

CHAPTER 17

Ralph Young looked up from his computer and saw Judd Slagle heading toward his desk. Instantly Ralph's mouth went dry, his heart raced and his eye twitched. Long sleepless nights had left him physically exhausted, and constant fear from Judd's threats had paralyzed his ability to think clearly. Ralph, once the bank's most prized worker, was now the brunt of jokes…behind his back, of course. He was forgetting the names of old customers, depositing money into the wrong accounts, and missing appointments.

By the time Judd reached his desk, Ralph was at the point of passing out. Expecting the worst, he was surprised when Judd walked by, and without even looking at him, dropped a plastic grocery bag into the wastebasket by the side of his desk. Ralph didn't move.

Behind him, he could hear Judd talking to Bill, the manager of the loan department. It was a short conversation and within minutes, Judd passed his desk on the way out.

Ralph tried to look nonchalant as he reached into the wastebasket, removed the plastic bag, and headed for the men's room. It was a good thing that all the stalls were empty because Ralph's reaction was explosive when the bloody head of his daughter's yellow striped cat rolled out of the bag.

When Ralph returned to his desk, his face was pasty white and his mouth tasted like vomit. Clutched in a shaking hand was a photograph that had been inside a separate plastic bag along with the cat's head. It was the picture Ralph's wife had used for their Christmas card the year before. His daughter was sitting across their laps grinning from ear to ear, the little yellow cat curled in her lap. A red 'X' blotted out the cat's head. On the back, "FIND THE COLLAR" was written in red.

Whatever color Ralph still had in his face drained away. The picture slipped from his fingers and tears trickled down his cheeks. He squeezed his eyes closed but the image of the dead cat and the warning on the photograph was etched on the back of his eyelids. He knew that this was just the beginning.

***

The truck with debris from Susan's house backed up to the area where the driver had been instructed to dump the load. As the bed was lowered, the contents of the truck slid off, and Susan's contribution was added to the growing city dump. The job finished, the driver attempted to raise the truck's bed but a grinding noise made him stop. It didn't take him long to find the problem; a very heavy and ornate animal collar had jammed the mechanism. His first reaction was to toss it on top of the pile he had just unloaded. On second thought, it looked expensive and since it hadn't sustained any damage, the driver stuck it in his pocket. Why not find a buyer for the collar?

CHAPTER 18

Julia watched her first period class file into the room and find their seats. As usual, Amelia was at the tail end of the line. Julia was noticing that the girl wasn't limping today and was equally surprised when Amelia raised her eyes and smiled. Things at home must have improved.

Amelia had expressed concern that the police had believed her dad when he told them that his daughter "told stories." Julia had talked to Officer Allen who assured her that Judd Slagle was the one they didn't believe. They were also convinced that Judd was responsible for the attack on Susan, but without any evidence, there wasn't much they could do about it.

Susan had recovered from the head injury, but yesterday something had happened that had sent her into an emotional tailspin. It had something to do with a man who had helped Denny with his stalled car. According to Denny, the man that he had taken to Susan's house to clean up must have turned around and left because he had just remembered another appointment. According to Susan, the man turned around and left because he had seen her. There had been something about the stranger that triggered Susan's reactions. She had prattled on about passing by the car where the stranger was having some emotional problem of his own.

Amelia, who had been standing quietly by Julia's desk waiting to be noticed, interrupted Julia's thoughts.

"Miss Cook?"

Julia jerked her head and looked up. "Oh, Amelia, do you want something?"

Amelia giggled. "No, I want to tell you something."

Julia was momentarily stunned by Amelia's radiant face. She would bet money that the child had no idea that she was beautiful.

"Well," Julia smiled back, "it must be something good!"

"It's the best!" the girl gushed. She paused for a heartbeat before she continued. "Dad...you know, he, ah, he, he doesn't always treat me very nice."

Julia nodded.

"He never remembers my birthday or anything like that, but I think maybe he's changed."

"What did he do?"

"I've wanted a pet ever since Mom died, but Dad wouldn't even talk to me about it. So I was surprised last night when he walked into the house with a yellow striped cat under his arm!"

"How wonderful!" Julia exclaimed.

"He had never said anything about getting me a cat. Miss Cook, do you think this means Dad is going to be nicer to me?"

Julia didn't want to rain on Amelia's parade, so she didn't answer the question. She just asked, "Where did he get the cat?"

"He said he got it from the pound."

"Have you given him a name?"

She shook her head. "Not yet. I'm waiting until I spend a few days with him to see what name fits him best."

"Sounds like a good idea. Where did he spend the night?"

"With me in my room!" Amelia's smiling face clouded. "He was there when I went to sleep, but this morning when I woke up, he was gone. I'm sure he's hiding somewhere in the house. I just didn't have time to look for him before I left for school."

"Well, let me know what you name him. And, I notice that you haven't been limping."

Amelia blushed. "You noticed before when I did?"

"Yes, Amelia, I noticed."

Amelia looked around to make sure no one was near enough to hear her whisper. "You know that Dad blocked the register so that I won't hear what's going on in his office. There are men there every night because I can see their cars out my window. Something is going on, but that's okay with me. Anything that takes Dad's attention away from me is good."

"Amelia, you do know that you can talk to me about anything," Julia said softly.

"I know," Amelia whispered, and then turned and went back to her seat.

***

Ralph left the bank and rushed to the refuge of his home. The day had been filled with troubling events and roller coaster emotions; the sight of the cat's head had shocked him to the core. How was he going to act when his daughter pleaded for him to help search for her lost cat...the cat whose head he had buried in the woods on the way home?

He was deep in thought when the sound of purring caught his attention. Stunned beyond words, he watched as his daughter's yellow striped cat circled around his feet.

Someone other than his daughter had lost a cat today.

***

Even though the register in Amelia's room had been closed, Judd could hear her wailing quite clearly.

She should have been in bed when he walked into the house last night carrying the cat, but as luck would have it, she was looking for a book she had left on the kitchen table. He'd never intended for her to see the cat, but she had. Grabbing it from him, she had cried tears of joy. For a brief second, he'd been horrified at the thought that she was going to hug him. When the moment passed, Amelia, with the cat in her arms, had run back to her room. He had waited for her to be asleep before he removed the cat from her bed.

Of course, the cat hadn't been there when she'd returned home from school. He had even helped her look for it, all the while knowing that there was no cat. He almost, but not quite, felt sorry for what he'd done. That feeling was so foreign, it had come and gone in the blink of an eye. In fact, he was getting pretty tired of the howling coming from her room. If she didn't shut up soon, he was going to go up there and give her something to howl about.

Chapter 19

Ryan looked at the mess he had made on his jacket sleeve where, despite his efforts, the oil stain remained. Desperate to find something that would get his mind off yesterday, he attacked the stain with renewed energy.

He hurt. That is the only way he could describe his feelings. Just seeing Susan yesterday had unleashed warm memories so full of love he grabbed them, relived them, and cherished them. He had never felt more alive than he had during those days they had spent together. How such love could develop in that short period didn't make sense, but it had. Life without her had no meaning, so why had he frozen yesterday when he'd had the chance to meet her in an unplanned situation? Now he had to find an accidental way to run into her again. The only way he knew how to get into her world was through real estate, but he had already done that. That's how he'd met her in the first place.

Sighing heavily, he poured himself a cup of coffee, settled himself at the table, picked up the morning paper, and stared at the unexpected sight of Susan's picture staring back at him. Her image sent a series of shock waves through his body. Stunned, he was unable to take his eyes off her face to read the verbiage under the picture. Fighting for control, he finally saw that she was standing by a sign stuck in the front yard of one of her listings. A smiling Susan was pointing to the OPEN SUNDAY sticker she had slapped on the for sale sign. He mentally noted the address of the house.

The first time he had worked with her, he'd posed as a transferee from Pittsburgh whose company was relocating him. This time he would have to come up with a reason why he, Keith, an investment banker, needed the help of a realtor. Since he had no idea what investment bankers did and he had no Internet to find out, he almost backed out of the idea of being one. Maybe he wouldn't get into trouble if he claimed to be a *retired* investment banker. Now, he'd go to a copy shop and have business cards made. Not having a phone number was another problem. He didn't have a number because he didn't have a landline phone, and since it had become too easy to trace someone's whereabouts through a cell phone, he didn't have one of those, either.

Later that day, he left the copy shop with a stack of business cards that proclaimed he was Keith Lambert, Investment Banker. The phone number listed on the card was just numbers.

***

With the trunk of her car loaded with open signs, her briefcase filled with informative flyers, a paperback book to read in case no one showed up, and a carrying case that contained the dog, Susan headed to Green Street for her Sunday afternoon open house.

As she stopped at each intersection feeding into Green Street to place an open sign with an arrow pointing in the direction of the house, she was thinking about the time she had sat down with a calculator and figured how many Sunday afternoons she had spent sitting in houses waiting for an interested buyer to show up. To that number, she compared how many of those visitors had actually bought that particular house. The answer was less than the fingers on one hand. Realtors hold open houses for several reasons. One is to show the seller that they are working to sell his property and another is to pick up customers. When it becomes apparent that the viewer isn't interested in the house, it's just a natural thing for the realtor to say, "Let me tell you about another house I think you would like. When would be a good time to show it to you?"

With the intersections taken care of, Susan drove to her listing. After setting up a sign by the driveway, she used her key to open the door. Professional cleaners had been hired to clean the mess left by the squatters. The smell of cleaning agents hit her nose as soon as she stepped into the foyer.

Susan was so intent on opening the window over the sink that she never heard the sound of a car pulling into the driveway. When a deep voice behind her asked, "May I help you with that?" she jumped back and had a second to enjoy the broad chest she had slammed into.

"Oof!" the deep voice of the man exclaimed as he frantically tried to regain his balance.

Susan whirled around in time to see a tall white-haired man lose the battle with gravity. A giggle was her immediate response to the sight of the handsome man staring up at her from his position on the floor.

Susan's laughing face, so close! Ryan couldn't breathe, he couldn't move, he couldn't speak.

Her face clouded. "I'm so sorry!" she exclaimed while holding out her hand. "How insensitive of me! Are you hurt?"

Strabismus, who had dozed off in his carrying case and was unaware that someone had come into the house, woke up in time to see his person about to share her hand with a stranger.

Strabismus' sharp bark startled Ryan. In a shaky voice that had nothing to do with the accident, he managed to say, "No, the only thing that's hurt is my pride. But tell me, is there an animal in the house?"

Susan chuckled. "Yes, there is, but you're safe! My dog is in a carrying case, and believe me, his bark is bigger than he is!"

Ryan's eyes looked around the room for the case, and when he found it, the two wandering eyes that were fighting to stare in his direction took him aback, and then he remembered; he had seen the dog before.

"Uh, about the dog…."

Susan raised her eyebrows. "What about the dog?"

Strabismus trilled.

"Is he looking at me? I really can't tell."

"That's because he's cross-eyed. His name is Strabismus."

Ryan chuckled. "Where on earth did you find a cross-eyed dog?"

"Right in this house," Susan informed him. "The squatters were kicked out, but when they left, they didn't take their dog with them. Aren't you getting uncomfortable sitting on the floor?"

Strabismus rewarded the question with a short burst of sound.

"A little help here?" Ryan grinned and held out his hand.

Susan fussed as she pulled him to his feet. "Thank goodness you aren't hurt! I had no idea anyone else was in the house. I was just trying to open a window to let in some fresh air."

110

Ryan was having trouble controlling his emotions. Susan was still holding his hand.

"...about the house?"

The dog almost harmonized with himself.

Realizing she had just asked him a question, he dropped her hand and jerked himself into the present. "Uh, you asked a question?"

"I just asked if you are interested in seeing an informative flyer about the house?"

Strabismus howled.

"You have one?"

"Yes, I do," Susan grabbed her briefcase and opened it. Handing a flyer to the man, she asked, "Is this house something you might be interested in?"

Puzzled, Ryan looked at the dog who had gone up and down the musical scale. "That's quite a vocal dog you have there."

Susan laughed. "For some reason, Strabismus either likes or doesn't like my voice when I ask a question. I claim he's singing."

"Just your voice?"

"I've had him for such a short time I don't really know. But as of now, mine is the only voice that makes him sing. I really have to learn to make statements and not ask questions."

Ryan grinned. "He might do well in a sing-off competition, but I sure wouldn't enter him in a beauty contest!"

The smile vanished from Susan's face. Before she could object to the man's criticism of her dog, he handed her a business card. "By the way, my name is Keith Lambert."

Susan's face brightened. "You!" she exclaimed with amusement. "It was you!"

Ryan knew what she was referring to but chose to play dumb.

"Me? What did I do?"

"You're the man who got his hand dirty helping Denny fix his car. He brought you to my house to be cleaned up, but you took one look at me and hightailed it out of there. You looked as if you'd seen a ghost…or a witch…or something."

Oh, boy. "Uh…that is… uh…I …you …yes, you… just seeing you made me remember that I had an appointment that I was going to miss if I took the time to clean up."

Susan, remembering the man in the parked car that Denny claimed was either laughing or crying, raised skeptical eyes. Lying, a new element, had just been added to the old mystery of why the man had run away.

"Oh well, you're here now," she paused in the middle of fanning the flyers in an arc on the kitchen counter. "I'm Susan Cook, the listing agent. The bank owns the house, in case you're interested. Feel free to look around."

"I'll do that!" he said, and headed toward the next room.

Susan glanced up, and for a brief second she got a glimpse of the back of the man as he disappeared into the next room. It surprised her when her heart skipped a beat. *What was that about?*

When Keith Lambert walked back into the kitchen, Susan was waiting for him with a sleeping dog in her arms. "Did you like what you saw?"

"It's not bad, but I m looking for something larger."

112

Susan opened her appointment book. "Let me tell you about another house I think you would like. When would be a good time to show it to you?"

CHAPTER 20

With the sound of the door closing behind the white-haired man, the house that had seemed so bright and full of life suddenly felt dark and dead. The thought of sitting in the house until three o'clock waiting for potential buyers was suddenly something she didn't want to do. If the open house hadn't been advertised in several local papers, she would've locked up and gone home. With a sigh of resignation, she settled in for a long afternoon until she remembered the book she'd grabbed from the pile in her den. Reading a book always made the time pass faster. With a book in her hand, she looked around for a place to sit. There was no furniture in the house, and since she hadn't thought to bring a folding chair, she had two choices. She could read the book standing up while leaning on the kitchen counter, or she could sit on the hard granite ledge extending out from the fireplace.

Glancing at her watch, she winced at the thought that she had two and a half hours before she could close the house and go home. Resigned to her fate, she sat down on the hard granite and opened the book, only to discover that she'd grabbed a book she'd already read.

It was going to be a long two and half hours. Strabismus, who had fallen asleep, woke up, and whined. Knowing that he had lived in the house for several days and hadn't had an accident, Susan felt confident that she could let him out of the cage.

With the dog on her lap and nothing else to do, her thoughts went to the white-haired man. She had been surprised, when she'd gotten a closer look at him that his face and his white hair hadn't gone together. What she had seen the day Denny brought him to her house was an old man with a limp. What she saw today was a handsome man, probably in his mid-forties.

For the time remaining, Susan mulled over the mystery that surrounded the man. Why had he run away from her, and why had he lied about the reason he'd run away?

There were no more visitors, so by three o'clock she was more than ready to put the dog back into the carrying case, close the house, pick up all the signs, and head for home. All she had to show for her three hours was an appointment with Keith Lambert to show him another house on Wednesday.

**

Ryan was having trouble breathing. He had been close, so close to her he could smell her, and surely close enough for her to hear the pounding of his heart. How could she not have felt the love that was pouring out of him? But she hadn't. He had watched her steady hand as she calmly wrote down their next scheduled appointment.

He made it to his car, and with a hand that wasn't steady, he tried three times before he was able to fit the key into the ignition. After he regained control, he slowly backed out of the driveway. The idea of keeping his identity from her was the last thing that he wanted to do. He wanted her to know who he was, but knew how shocked she was going to be when she found out that Ryan Wilcox was very much alive.

He needed a plan.

What if…what if Keith Lambert courted her? Could he make Susan fall in love again, only this time with Keith?

CHAPTER 21

Julia stood by her open door and greeted the eighth-graders as they filed past her on their way to their seats. She was about to close the door when the sight of a slight girl limping toward her made her catch her breath. It was Amelia.

The last bell had rung but Susan stayed by the door until Amelia made it to the room. Neither one said a word as Julia's tear-filled eyes searched Amelia's pain-filled ones.

"Your dad?" Julia asked.

Amelia refused to meet her teacher's eyes.

"Want to tell me about it?"

The girl shook her head.

Julia tried another subject.

"Did you name your cat?"

Amelia's pain-filled eyes now had tears in them.

"There is no cat."

"No cat?"

"When I got home from school yesterday, I looked for the cat, but he was gone. I cried."

"Of course you cried! But why are you limping?"

Amelia looked at the floor.

"Oh, Amelia, you have to talk to someone! I can't close my eyes and pretend nothing is happening!"

"Miss Cook," Amelia pleaded, "unless you can protect me from my dad, don't even think about reporting him. You haven't seen his face when he's angry, but I have. He'd kill me."

Julia shook her head. "You'd be protected from him because you wouldn't be living under his roof anymore."

"It wouldn't matter, Miss Cook. He'd find me." She took a deep breath and whispered, "I know what happened to the cat."

"Something happened to the cat?"

Amelia nodded.

"You're referring to the cat that you thought your dad had brought home for you?"

She nodded again.

"What happened?"

"Garbage pickup is today, and one of my jobs is to haul the full can up to the road. I'd never raised the lid to look at what was in the can before, but for some reason today, I did." Amelia paused, and swallowed hard. "Miss Cook, right on top was the headless body of the yellow cat."

Julia was so upset by Amelia's cat story that she didn't trust her voice. Instead, she was trying to keep her hand steady enough to write an assignment on the board. She knew that what she was asking her class to do was just busy work, something that she swore she'd never do. But this

118

was an emergency. She had to leave her room unsupervised while she ran to the office to tell Mrs. Sheldon the cat story.

She was going to accuse Judd Slagle of child abuse, and Amelia was going to need a safe place to hide.

***

Holding an ornate dog collar in his hand, the owner of the pet store watched the disappointed man stuff a ten-dollar bill into his pocket and leave the store. Granted, the uniquely crafted collar was worth much more than he had given the man, but the shop owner was doubtful if any of his customers would be interested in putting such an ornate and heavy collar around their dog's neck.

But the collar was definitely an eye-catcher, something that others might enjoy checking out, and maybe, just maybe, bring them into his store.

With that in mind, he found a piece of black velvet, placed the collar on it, and put it on display in the store's window.

CHAPTER 22

It was late Wednesday afternoon, and according to her schedule, Susan had an appointment to show Keith Lambert a house. For the first time since returning home from the Incident, she was actually looking forward to going back to work. She didn't know why, but the urge to be back at her own house sitting on the swing with the fur coat wrapped around, waiting for Ryan's return was gone.

Ryan, who had requested the late appointment, was already parked in the driveway of the scheduled house when Susan arrived. Just watching her park her car behind his car gave him a warm feeling of impending intimacy; his heart felt as if it were expending in his chest. He opened the door and stepped out. The sight of his smiling Susan walking toward him carrying the dog cage took his breath away. Today was the day he would start the courting process that would end with Susan falling in love with Keith Lambert. He hadn't quite figured out how he would turn her love for Keith Lambert back to him, Ryan Wilcox. When the time came, he'd worry about it, but now was the time to bask in the sunshine that radiated from his beloved Susan.

Even though Ryan had no interest in the house, he managed to chatter enthusiastically about its good points. Staying close to her side, he commented on each room, having something positive to say, all the while entertaining her with clever conversation. The sound of laughter followed them through the house. Having Strabismus howl after every question Susan asked added to the party atmosphere. Then, when at the end of the tour he announced that he wasn't going to buy the house, Susan stammered, "B…b…but…!"

"Well, maybe I will buy it, but what if there's a house out there that's better than this one?"

"You want to see more houses?"

Strabismus sang.

"I believe that's what I said."

"But you asked for certain features in a house. There are no more houses on the market with those particular amenities."

"What do we do, then?"

Susan's grin was forced. "Other than building one yourself, I guess you'll just have to wait."

He stared off into space, giving the impression he was thinking very seriously about the problem. "I'm really not in a hurry to buy just anything, so I'm not unhappy that I have to wait." Ryan paused to look down into Susan's upturned puzzled face. His legs turned to jelly, his mouth went dry, and his voice sounded adolescent when he asked, "Uh, Mrs. Cook, uh, would you like…uh, since it's late in the day, that is, uh, would you consider having dinner with me?"

Susan's eyes swept over the handsome man who was looking intently down at her. Go to dinner with him? Of course not! She couldn't go to dinner with him or any other man. What would Ryan think if he came back and saw her with someone else?

"Thank you for the invitation, Mr. Lambert. I do appreciate it, but I have to decline."

Ryan's jaw dropped. This was going to be harder than he thought.

"I have your business card," she told him. "I'll call you when a similar house comes on the market."

Susan held her tongue, because she wanted to add, "...but don't hold your breath." According to the list of things the buyer wanted in a house, this one had them all. On top of that, the location was wonderful, the landscaping was professional, and the interior was outstanding. The chance that a better one would come on the market was slim. What a waste of her time! Instead of working with buyers, maybe she should just stick to listing houses.

With that, she locked up the house, and without looking back at him, walked to her car.

Her last words to him, "I'll call you when a similar house comes on the market," rang in his ears. Putting a made-up phone number on his business card hadn't been such a good idea. Sick at heart, he watched her drive away.

He leaned against his car, placed his elbows on the roof, and covered his face with his hands. This was not the ending he had envisioned. Not even close. In fact, he either had to cancel the dinner reservation or show up and eat alone. His rumbling stomach helped him make a decision. He'd eat alone.

The Collar

Finding an empty parking spot across the street from the restaurant, he got out of the car, locked it, and then headed in the direction of the entrance. His mind was spinning. Since he couldn't take the chance she'd try to call him on the fake numbers on his business card, he had to come up with a reason to drop into her office when she was on duty.

While passing the town's only pet store, a very ornate collar displayed in the front window caught his eye. From what he could see, it was an exceptionally well-crafted piece of art created for a large dog. Flowers were too obvious, perfume was too personal, and a funny card might offend her. But a dog collar, even if it was too big for her dog, might be so nonsensical that he just might get away with it. He was desperate. Perhaps someday, after the two of them were married and dining by candlelight, they could look back and laugh about his incongruous gift.

A quick glance at his watch assured him that he could make the purchase and still be on time for his reservation.

***

Susan gazed out the window of her motel room with unseeing eyes. Unexplained emotions and impatient feelings about something puzzled her. What they were, she had no idea, but the strong sense of certainty that she should be somewhere other than in the motel room nagged at her. Her stomach rumbled. Maybe she should have taken Julia and Denny's invitation to have dinner with them at his house. It was wonderful that her daughter had found love, but being a first-hand witness to their affectionate displays was painful. Was turning down their invitation the reason she was feeling so displaced? With a resigned sigh, she gave up trying to figure it out.

Keith Lambert's invitation to dinner was so unimportant; she never gave it another thought.

CHAPTER 23

Susan and her real estate partner, Zena, were at the end of their two-hour stint at the front desk when Emma, the secretary, called to them. "An interested buyer wants to talk to a realtor. Whose turn is it?"

It had been a slow two hours and Susan and Zena had time to catch up on all the happenings since the last time they had shared floor duty. Zena's youngest had hit the Terrible Twos and his antics were the source of several amusing stories. That also explained the bags under Zena's eyes.

Zena shook her head. "It's my turn, but I don't want another buyer right now. I'm hanging on by my fingernails just to get through floor duty. All I can think about right now is going home and hitting the couch. Susan, it's yours."

Susan picked up the phone. "Susan Cook here. What property were you calling about?"

When it became apparent from one end of the conversation that the property the caller was interested in had been sold, Zena watched her partner skillfully corral the caller into considering another one of their listings. It must have worked, because Susan grabbed her purse, picked up the dog's carrying case, waved goodbye to Zena, and was running for the door, when it opened.

"Oof!" she exclaimed, as she bounced off the man's chest.

"Oof, yourself," Ryan grinned as he looked down at her.

"Oh, Keith, it's you!" Susan exclaimed. "Sorry about running into you again!"

Still smiling, he replied, "At least you didn't knock me down this time."

"I'm in a bit of a hurry," she exclaimed, stepping around him.

"I can see that!"

"Uh, did you need something?" she paused when she was halfway out the door. "I told you I'd call you when another house came on the market."

"I know you did, but that's not why I stopped in to see you." He held up a brightly wrapped object.

Susan looked warily at the parcel. "Is that something for me?"

There was a sparkle in his eye as he brandished it under her nose. "Curious?"

"Well, it's not my birthday, so I have no idea why you would be giving me a present. Tell you what. Give it to Zena and she can put it on my desk. I'll call you when I get back!"

With a wave of her hand, she ran to her car.

Ryan watched in dismay as her car pulled out of the parking lot and merged with traffic. Just thinking about Susan trying to call the bogus phone number on his card was so upsetting, he hardly noticed when Zena took the package out of his hand and walked off with it.

126

So much for the plan. Once again, this was not the ending he'd envisioned.

***

For the next couple of days, Ryan's mood fluctuated between giddiness and dread. How Susan had reacted to his gift was keeping him awake at night. If she saw humor in the large dog collar, the two of them could share a laugh, but since she hadn't responded one way or another, he had the awful feeling she'd found nothing amusing in the inappropriate present. Then again, the fake number would result in no response whatsoever if he couldn't arrange another meeting with her. Berating his poor judgment, he was wondering what his next courting step would be when, while driving back from town, he saw a new for sale sign on a very attractive but very different kind of house. He'd have to come up with a reason why he wanted to see it.

The sound of Susan's voice when he heard, "Town and Country Real Estate. How may I help you?" sent chills up and down his spine.

"Hi Susan!" Ryan managed to say in spite of a dry mouth and a tongue that didn't want to work.

Susan hesitated. She hated people who called and assumed that she would recognize their voice. Come to think of it, the voice did sound familiar.

"Mr. Lambert?"

Ryan took a deep breath. So now he was Mr. Lambert? Not even a friendly Keith? He had an urge to deny her assumption and hang up, but he didn't.

"Uh, yes it is," he answered.

"How may I help you?"

"I'm calling about a newly listed house on Crooks Road. Are you familiar with it?"

"That's Allen Real Estate's new listing, and no, I'm not familiar with it. Why do you ask?"

"It looks interesting."

Susan didn't say anything for a moment while she looked up the information on the new listing. "That's a nice house, but it doesn't have any of the amenities that you said were important."

Ryan managed to work a chuckle into his voice. "Am I allowed to change my mind?"

"Sure you are! I'm always surprised when I compare what buyers actually purchased to what they'd asked for in the beginning. Would you like to see it?"

"Yes, I would. When could you do it?"

"I'm tied up for the rest of the day, but you can still see it. The listing realtor, Molly Allen Hatch, is holding it open today between one o'clock and three o'clock. I'll call Molly and tell her one of my customers will be dropping in to see the house."

"But you won't be showing me the house?"

"Oh, if you decide you want to buy it, we certainly will go back and do a closer inspection. Another call is coming in, so I have to go. Thanks for calling, Mr. Lambert."

Ryan was left with a dead phone and an open mouth. Once again, this was not how he'd envisioned the end of the call.

It wasn't until much later that he remembered she hadn't mentioned the gift.

CHAPTER 24

Ralph Young was just a shadow of his former self. Sleepless nights were bad, but the nightmares that occurred on the rare occasion that he did manage to fall asleep were worse. The cat's head had destroyed him. Judd Slagle's demand that he find the collar had sent him to hell and back with the threat of another visit to the fiery pits. He had no idea where to look. Fear for his family hung over him like a black cloud. His wife, who had figured that something terrible was going on, was threatening to leave him if he continued to shut her out. Since he had broken many covenants of his church, he not only resigned as an elder, he had completely stopped attending services. The last blow was when he was called into his employer's office and was told that if things didn't improve, especially in his handling of the bank's real estate holdings, he would no longer have a job.

Ralph pulled himself together enough to tackle the problem. After his regular banking duties were covered for the day, his new schedule included visiting one of the properties that had reverted to the bank. If it had been put back on the market, he checked to see if the realtor who had been given the listing was doing a good job. Tomorrow, it was the house on Green Street that he would check. He would visit Susan Cook at Town and Country Real Estate.

After another nightmare-filled night, Ralph avoided looking at himself in the mirror. Not wanting his superior to see his shaky hands, his jerking head and his bloodshot eyes, he had found refuge in the bank's main restroom. His boss, who had his own private restroom, would never think to look for him here. But just to be safe, he dashed into a stall when he heard the door being opened. Holding his breath, he listened as the sound of footsteps came closer and closer.

It wasn't his employer's voice that whispered, "Ralphie baby? I know you're in there. Do you really think you can hide from me? I'm not waiting much longer! I WANT THAT COLLAR!"

Ralph vomited.

From his position on the floor, he could see Judd Slagle's feet finally move away from his stall. The sound of the door being opened and closed told Ralph that he was alone. Choking sobs racked his body as fear stole the breath from his lungs. What was he going to do? It was his fault that his family was in danger. When Anna had given him the envelope with Amelia's name on it, the instructions were that Judd was never to find out what was in it. Ralph had always thought that he was a strong and principled man; finding out that he was neither strong nor principled shook him to the very core of his soul. How weak he was!

He didn't deserve to live.

The thought of suicide broadsided him. Never before in his life had he entertained the thought of taking his own life, but now that he had, he grabbed onto the idea much like a drowning man would seize an offered hand; there would be no reason for Judd to touch his family if he were out of the picture. Unbidden, the image of opening a package, and instead of a cat's head rolling out, it was his daughter's....

Ralph vomited again.

Thoughts of his immortal soul burning in the everlasting fire of Hell brought him up short. Suicide, according to Ralph's beliefs, was a sin. There had to be another way. He needed to talk to someone. His pastor had been upset with him when he resigned his position as an elder, but aren't ministers supposed to share God's unconditional love with their flock? He really didn't want to reveal the sordid details of his fall from grace, and maybe he wouldn't have to.

Ralph looked at his watch. Alarmed at the length of time he'd hidden in the men's room, he left the stall, rinsed his mouth, splashed water on his face, and headed back to his office. As he passed the front desk, the receptionist looked up from her computer long enough to call to him.

"Mr. Young?

"Yes?"

"There's a gentleman waiting for you in your office."

"Did he give you his name?"

"Uh," she looked around her desk. "Oh, here it is. He gave me his card. It's Mr. Judd Slagle."

On the outside, he retained his composure. On the inside, he was screaming. Without missing a beat, he turned around and headed for the door. "I'm gone for the day," he called back over his shoulder.

"But what will I tell Mr. Slagle?"

With his hand on the handle, Ralph paused long enough to reply, "You're a bright girl...make up something!"

Running as if his life depended on it, Ralph didn't slow down until he had arrived at the familiar door of the church. The last conversation he'd had with his friend, Reverend Joe, hadn't ended well. Even over the phone, he could tell that Joe was picking up the stress in his voice. His pride had kept him from sharing his sordid problem, but now, when thoughts of suicide as the solution to his predicament were growing stronger by the minute, things had changed.

Within moments of entering the sanctuary, the sound of the organ playing a familiar hymn brought him to his knees. How could he even consider separating himself from the love of God by taking his own life? And then, unbidden, once again came the image of his daughter's head rolling out of a plastic bag.

Expecting to see Reverend Joe sitting behind his desk, he felt disheartened when he found the office empty. Following the sound of a vacuum cleaner that was competing with the organ music, Ralph found a maintenance worker whose ears were plugged with buds that were connected to an iPod in his pocket. Ralph's tap on the shoulder made him jump.

"Jeez!"

"Sorry about that!" Ralph said after the worker removed the buds from his ears and turned off the machine.

"You want something?"

"I'm looking for Reverend Joe, but he's not in his office. Do you know where he is?"

"Somewhere out of state," the worker replied as he turned back to his machine. Before he could turn it on, Ralph stopped him.

"Wait a minute! Where is he?"

"He was on the phone this morning when I came in, and I heard him say something about officiating at a relative's funeral."

Ralph's heart sank. He was depending on his friend and pastor to talk him out of doing what he sensed was the only way to protect his family.

As he headed to the sanctuary and the familiar family pew, the grating sound of the vacuum was replaced by soothing organ music. Sitting in the same seat that had been, until recently, a place of comfort and peace, he was finding it difficult to entertain thoughts of suicide. How could he sit here making plans to end his life? There had to be another way.

That's when he remembered the suicide prevention hot line.

Moments later, Ralph put his phone back into his pocket and walked out of the church. The final straw was hearing that the suicide counselor was at the bridge trying to talk some guy out of jumping. A fleeting thought that he and the jumper could hold hands and leap together was so ludicrous, he almost smiled. How was he going to commit the awful deed was the question. Hanging himself in his office would be better than doing it at home. The thought of his daughter finding his body was unacceptable. He hoped no one was watching when he dry-heaved into a bush next to the sidewalk.

The planning went on in his head as he continued walking. Noticing that he was near Town and Country Real Estate, he decided that the last thing he would do in this life would be to check in with Susan Cook, the realtor who had the listing on the Green Street house. He briefly wondered how she would feel tomorrow when she heard about his suicide.

With thoughts of death whirling through his head, he entered the real estate office to find that there was no one at the reception desk. That was all right, because he knew where he was going. No one paid any attention to him as he made his way past salespeople who held phones to their ears.

Finding her office empty was just another blow. Nothing was going right this last day of his life. Maybe he should leave her a note that he'd been here to check on the bank's property. At least his employer would know that he'd been responsible to the bitter end. Yes, that's what he'd do; he'd leave a note.

Mrs. Cook was a nice lady who, he was sure, wouldn't object to his looking in her desk for a piece of paper and a pen.

He didn't mean to do it, but in his haste, he knocked a brightly wrapped package off her desk. It hit the floor with a solid thunk, which told him that it contained something other than glass. Feeling thankful for the small favor, he bent over and picked it up. The package had ripped open in the fall, and as he stared past the bright paper, he realized he was looking at his Holy Grail.

He'd found the collar.

***

Tired of waiting in Ralph Young's office, Judd Slagle was making his way to the bank's front entrance when he saw Ralph abruptly change directions. The speed at which Ralph exited the bank made Judd grin. He had no reason to doubt that the receptionist had told Ralph who was waiting for him in his office. Fear always worked for Judd.

By the time Judd was out on the street, there was no sign of Ralph. Knowing that he couldn't have gone very far, Judd got into his car and slowly drove up and down the street until he sighted Ralph coming out of the Presbyterian Church. The man looked so dejected and beaten, Judd almost felt sorry for him. The fleeting emotion turned to surprise when Ralph disappeared into a real estate office, only to appear minutes later clutching something in his hand. The dejected and beaten man who had gone into the real estate office wasn't dejected and beaten any longer. In fact, he was laughing hysterically. Finding the collar was the only thing that would make Ralph laugh that way.

Judd had to find a parking place, and by the time he did, Ralph had run into the police station.

"No!" Judd cried to no one in particular. "No!"

CHAPTER 25

Julia left the meeting with Officer Tom Allen and Detective Mitch Hatch feeling as if a load had been lifted off her shoulders. Judd wouldn't be contacted until they had a safe place for Amelia to hide. The girl never would admit to her that her father had caused the injuries, and she'd probably do the same thing when questioned by anyone else, but Julia couldn't ignore the headless cat incident. Why Judd had done something so horrible was a mystery, but just knowing he was capable of such cruelty was enough for Julia to go against Amelia's pleadings. What would happen now was out of her hands.

Before Julia left, the subject had come up about the dog collar that she'd misplaced and the suspicion that Judd Slagle had wanted it badly enough to assault Susan and trash her house. Julia was relieved to hear that Amelia's account was believed even though Judd had insisted that his daughter "told stories." As far as anyone knew, the collar had never resurfaced.

Coming in as she left the building was a wild-looking man whose bloodshot eyes and a facial tic caused her to hastily step aside to let him pass.

***

Detective Hatch and Officer Allen were discussing Julia's child-abuse accusation against Judd Slagle when the door to the office flew open and a man, obviously high on something, burst into the room.

Before either had the chance to object, the man tossed a large ornate dog collar onto the desk as if it were burning his fingers.

"Here, you take it," he cried. "Just watch out for Judd Slagle because he's willing to kill for the message hidden inside it!"

Surprised, the two men realized that the collar on the desk had to be the one Julia had lost and the reason Susan's house had been ransacked.

When Officer Allen tore his eyes away from the elusive collar to take a good look at the distressed man who had delivered it, he exclaimed, "I recognize you! You work at the bank, don't you?"

Struggling to get himself under control, Ralph nodded. "M… my name is," he swallowed hard and tried again. "My name is Ralph Young, and I'm in charge of the mortgage department. It's a small bank and we all have multiple jobs."

"Well, your job right now is explaining how you got your hands on that collar," Officer Allen demanded, pointing at the collar. "Have you had it all this time?"

Ralph lowered his bloodshot eyes. "No, I just found it, and to save my soul, I need to tell you everything."

The sour smell of vomit coming from Ralph was strong.

"Uh, Mr. Young, why don't you go to the restroom and freshen up? We'll have a cup of coffee waiting for you when you come back."

Ralph's grin was weak, but it was a grin. "I'll be right back. Oh, a little sugar and cream in the coffee, please?"

A much better-smelling and calmer Ralph emptied the cup and held it up for a refill before he started talking. He started with what he knew about Judd's mother and wife and his own violation of the trust the women had placed in him, and he finished with the confession that he had intended to take his own life. Finding the collar on Susan Cook's desk was completely unexpected.

The two men listened in awed silence. It was just thirty minutes ago that they'd first heard about the headless cat in the garbage can, and here was Ralph telling them the rest of the story. The collar, however, had brought several new mysteries: how it had disappeared from Susan's house, where had it gone, who had found it, who had gift-wrapped it and who had placed the collar on Susan's desk.

How they were going to keep the knowledge from Judd Slagle was a matter of concern. The urge to throw his sorry ass in jail was strong, but the two officers couldn't come up with a reason that would stand up in court. While animal cruelty is a felony, the evidence was long gone. There was no proof that he was behind the trashing of Susan's house, the threats against Ralph were verbal and not in writing, and Amelia's refusal to implicate her dad wasn't helping.

Convinced that Judd Slagle would stop at nothing to find the location of the hidden wealth, they all agreed that anyone who knew the content of the message in the collar was in danger. Ralph was adamant in his demand that his family be protected. Explaining that he had actually run out of the bank when the receptionist informed him that Judd was waiting for him in his office, Ralph expressed his fear that Judd had been there either to make new threats or to strengthen the old ones. Either way, Ralph feared for his wife and daughter, and before he retrieved the message from the collar, he demanded that his family be put into protective custody.

After calls were made and his wife and daughter were tucked safely away in a secure house, Officer Allen and Detective Hatch watched Ralph pick up the collar.

CHAPTER 26

Susan studied the menu at the Omelet Shop all the while wondering why she was even bothering. She could probably recite it word for word if anyone ever asked her to, which, of course, no one ever would. The sound of laughter caused her to raise her eyes from the menu to look for the source. The first thing she saw was the radiant face of the young woman operating the cash register. Evidentially the gentleman paying his bill had said something that made her laugh. That drew Susan's eyes to the man who had his back turned toward her.

It was Ryan!

Susan gasped. Ryan had come back! Her head was spinning as she slid out of the booth and ran toward the front of the shop.

Having paid the bill, Ryan was pushing the door open to leave the shop when he felt a tap on his shoulder. Turning around, he was surprised to see Susan's beaming face dissolve quickly into one of despair.

To him, it felt like a physical blow when, with her voice full of regret, she managed to say, "Oh, it's you, Keith."

"Well, hello Susan! You sound disappointed. Did you think I was someone else?"

"Well, yes I did. From the back you look like…you look like, uh, you look like…uh, yes." She swallowed hard before she added, "You look like someone I used to know."

The sadness in Susan's face broke his heart. The idea to make Susan fall in love with Keith Lambert might have been a good one, but it wasn't working.

Putting a finger under Susan's chin, he raised her head so that he could look her in the eye. "Susan, would you have a cup of coffee with me, please? I need to tell you something really important."

Before Susan had time to reply, the door flew open and Officer Allen stepped in. "Oh, there you are, Mrs. Cook. I've been looking for you."

"Me?"

"Yes, you."

"Did I do something wrong," Susan looked distressed.

Ryan stepped in. "Just wait a minute, here. If you're bringing some kind of charge against this woman, I demand to know what it is."

Susan frowned. "You what? I don't even know you."

Ryan took her hand. "That's what I need to talk to you about."

Officer Allen stepped between the two of them. "Whatever it is that you need to talk to her about will have to wait. Mrs. Cook, please come with me."

Susan sputtered. "Are you arresting me?"

The officer chuckled. "No, no, nothing of the sort. We just have to ask you a couple of questions."

"B…but" Ryan objected.

"There are no buts about it. This is police business. If you have something to tell Mrs. Cook, you can tell her later."

A deflated Ryan watched as the love of his life ran back to her booth, grabbed the dog's cage, and walked off with the police officer. The timing had been so right!

***

"I don't understand," Susan protested while setting the dog cage that contained a sleeping Strabismus in an adjoining room. "You're telling me that the collar was in the wrapped package that I never opened?"

Ralph nodded. "I was looking for paper and a pen to leave you a message when I knocked it to the floor. When the wrapping split open, I saw the collar."

"And Judd Slagle wants the collar badly enough to trash my house and threaten you and your family? Is anyone going to tell me what's so special about it?" Susan demanded.

When no one offered an explanation, Susan threw up her hands. "So, it's a big secret?"

Officer Allen nodded. "It's a secret that you're better off not knowing."

Susan looked puzzled. "It's just a dog collar, isn't it?"

"It's more than just a collar, Susan. A hidden compartment had a message in it. Anyone knowing what's in the message is in danger."

"Danger? What kind of danger, and from whom?"

"Judd Slagle is willing to kill for the secret."

Since Ralph Young had given her the listing on Green Street, she knew that he worked in the mortgage department at the bank. "So let me get this straight. Whatever this big secret is, you put it in the dog's collar?"

"It wasn't like that at all!" Ralph protested. "Judd's mother had a dog that she rescued from the pound. No one wanted it because it was ugly and cross-eyed."

Ralph stopped talking when Susan cleared her throat. "Something wrong?" he asked.

"Not really." Retrieving her dog from the adjacent room, she placed the cage on a desk. "Meet Strabismus."

The dog's wandering eyes recognized his old owner; he growled.

"You have the dog now? Well, good luck! He's a yappy dog that can't stand to be alone for a minute."

Susan nodded. "I found that out real soon!"

Detective Hatch's head jerked when his eyes landed on the dog that was staring at him.

Ralph chuckled at the detective's reaction. "Hey, I told you he was ugly!"

"Enough already!" barked Hatch. "Mr. Young, get back to the subject!"

Ralph cleared his throat and continued. "Minnie, that's the name of Judd's mother, loved the dog. She got to know and trust me when I helped her and Judd's wife open a bank account and rent a safety-deposit box. She asked me if I'd take her dog upon her death. Oh, and the collar around the dog's neck? She made me promise that I'd keep it on the dog. I thought it was just an old woman's whim, but I left it on, even though the dog didn't like it. So, no, I didn't put the message in the collar. The women did that."

"I thought the squatters had left the dog in the house when the bank kicked them out. But that's not what happened, is it?"

When the dog sang several lines, Susan picked up the cage, put him back in the next room, and shut the door.

To answer the raised eyebrows, Susan explained. "Strabismus reacts to my voice when I ask a question. Believe me, I just did you all a favor."

Ralph lowered his eyes. "To answer your question, I'm the one who locked him in."

Three pair of eyes focused on Ralph.

"Okay, I'm not proud of what I did! The two women wanted all the wealth they had accumulated to go to Amelia. Not wanting Judd to get his hands on it, the women hid it. They wanted to tell me where it was hidden, but I wouldn't let them. They'd told me terrible stories about Judd, and I was scared if he found out that I knew where they had hidden it, he'd get it out of me. So, after Minnie's death, Anna gave me an envelope with Amelia's name on it. Inside the envelope, she told me, there was a message."

Ralph stopped talking. Knowing it was time to confess didn't make it any easier.

"The two women trusted me completely. What I did...well, I'm ashamed to admit that I broke their trust. Judd knew there were assets somewhere and he figured that I knew where they were. When he threatened me and my family...."

Pausing a moment to regain his composure, Ralph continued. "That's when I handed Judd the envelope."

"And?" Susan was leaning toward Ralph, hanging onto his every word.

"Judd ripped the envelope open and yelled, 'What the hell does this mean? It says to look inside the dog's collar. What collar? What dog?'"

"Oh," Susan declared. "Now it's all starting to make sense."

"I'll bet Judd didn't even know his mother had a dog," Officer Allen commented.

Ralph snorted. "There had been no contact between Judd and his mother for years. She was scared to death of him."

Susan threw both hands up. "Wait a minute!" she cried. "Why didn't you just take the dumb collar off the dog and hand it to Judd? I don't understand why you made such a big production out of it. Anyhow, it was a cruel thing you did…locking the poor dog in a vacant house."

"Poor dog, indeed. My neighbors constantly complained about the yappy dog, so I wanted to get rid of him. But the main reason was that I didn't want to have any further contact with Judd. The bank had just taken over the house on Green Street, so I handed Judd the key and told him the dog would be there."

Susan interrupted. "But I found the dog before Judd did. I took him home, and my daughter, Julia, somehow lost the collar. So, how did it leave my house?"

"And where did it go, who found it, and who wrapped it up as a gift?" Detective Hatch added.

"Oh, I can answer one of those questions," Susan claimed. "It was Keith Lambert, one of my customers, who wrapped it up as a gift and gave it to me."

"And where did he get the collar?" Officer Allen queried. "You had the collar to begin with, so why was he giving it back to you as a present?'

"Keith didn't know anything about the collar. I never told him."

"The man who was with you at the Omelet Shop…was that Keith?" Officer Allen asked. "Didn't he say he had something he wanted to talk to you about?"

"Yes, he did, but I have no idea what that's about. I hardly know the man. I met him at an open house, and when he didn't like the house, I showed him one more. That's all the contact I've had with him."

"And yet he was giving you a dog collar as a present? Had he ever seen the size of your dog?"

Susan thought. "Yes, he saw Strabismus at the open house where I first ran into him. He had to know the collar was too big, but why would he be giving me a dog collar in the first place? I admit he has shown interest in me…well, he did ask me out for dinner once. But if he wanted to impress me, why would he give me a dog collar? What ever happened to flowers and perfume?"

"We need to find him. Do you know how to reach him?"

"Of course I do! Do you think I'd let a buyer get away without any contact information?" Susan laughed.

Detective Hatch grinned. "I see your signs all over the town, so I'll bet that you do have his number."

"I have more than his number," Susan boasted. "I have his card."

The detective looked at the card. "Says here he's an investment banker. What does an investment banker do?"

Officer Allen, who was sitting at the computer, pulled up the Internet, typed in Investment Banking, and read. "'Investment bankers are generally very well-paid individuals, but these positions require specific skills, such as number-crunching ability, excellent verbal and written communication ability, and the capacity to work very long and gru....'"

Detective Hatch threw up his hands. "Enough already! Susan, looks like you have a buyer with lots of money. Now find him for us, please."

With a smile full of confidence, Susan dialed the number on the card. The men, watching her face, saw the smile of confidence fade, and by the time she hung up, she was frowning. "The operator says that's not a working number."

"Did you dial it right?" Officer Allen asked.

Handing him the business card, she said, "Here, you try."

No one said anything after Officer Allen hung up. "Did this Keith Lambert tell you where he was staying?"

Susan shook her head. "I guess I'm not such a great business woman after all."

Officer Allen stood up and headed for the inner office. "I'm putting an all-points bulletin out for Keith Lambert. All motels and hotels will be checked. Susan, can you give us a description?"

"Well, you saw him. What did you see?"

"I saw a tall good-looking man with white hair. Did I miss anything?"

"He has a slight limp, but that's the only thing I can add to the description," Susan replied. "Oh, he's a much younger man than his white hair leads you to believe. I would put him in his mid-forties."

Susan stuck around for a bit, watching the activities as the search for Keith Lambert went into full gear. She was about to leave when she heard Officer Allen ending a phone conversation with the words, "Good job!"

"Officer Allen, did your people find Keith?"

He shook his head. "There's no Keith Lambert registered anywhere in town. However, from our description, we've found where the guy had been staying. I say 'had been' because he checked out. Looks like he's left the area."

"If he didn't register under the name Keith Lambert, what name did he use?"

"Uh, here it is...I wrote it down. He registered under the name Charles Holiday."

Susan fainted.

CHAPTER 27

Julia rushed into the police station with fear in her heart. What had her mother gotten herself into this time? It wasn't long ago that Susan's life had been turned upside-down after she met Charles Holiday. She survived an attack on her home, a plane crash, and managed to stay alive for a few days lost in the middle of nowhere. The man who claimed to be Charles Holiday had pretended to be a buyer. His real name was Ryan Wilcox, a man with a price on his head who was running to stay alive. Ryan's enemies found him, and Susan, who had fallen in love with him, had returned home alone with a broken heart. Ryan was dead to everyone but Susan.

Julia had received the cell phone call in the middle of her third period American History class. Officer Allen had informed her that her mother needed her, and would she please come to the police station.

"The police station?" she questioned.

It took a collected gasp from the students to remind her where she was. She turned her body and lowered her voice.

"Right now?"

"Your mother fainted, and yes, I think you should come right now."

"Is she getting medical help?"

"We aren't equipped here at the station to handle serious injuries, but unless she hit her head, she should be waking up."

"You said, should be. Does that mean she hasn't?"

"No, she hasn't."

"What are they doing about it?"

"They're talking about taking her to the hospital."

"I can't just walk out of my classroom," Julia wailed. "Where am I going to get a sub to take over...oh, hello, Mrs. Sheldon!"

Mrs. Sheldon hurried into the room. "Miss Cook, I was hoping to get to you before Officer Allen called, but I can see that didn't happen. I'll take over your room, so be on your way."

"Oh, thank you, Mrs. Sheldon!"

Julia grabbed her purse and ran out of the room.

Seeing the ambulance outside the police station and knowing it was there for her mother, Julia had a moment of panic. Officer Allen met her at the door of the police station.

"Your mother is in here. She hasn't moved since she fainted, but her blood pressure is good and her breathing is steady."

"And why did she faint?" Julia asked. "What was going on?"

Officer Allen shrugged. "Not much. We were trying to find one of her buyers just to ask him a question. That's all."

"There has to be more to it than that!" Julia exclaimed. "Who is the buyer?"

"That's a good question. He'd told your mother that his name was Keith Lambert, but as it turned out, that wasn't his real name."

"Well, finish the story, for heaven's sake! What is his real name?"

"Charles Holiday."

"Oh, my God!"

Officer Allen raised his eyebrows. "Uh, I take it that the name Charles Holiday means something to your mother?"

"Oh, my God!"

"Miss Cook, you've already said that!"

"Oh, my...."

"Miss Cook, settle down! Why would that name have such an affect on your mother?"

Could it be? What were the chances that her mother had picked up another buyer with that name? Julia knew that just hearing the name had caused her mother to faint. If this Keith Lambert was really Ryan, why hadn't her mother recognized him? Denny had run into the man, and had even brought him to the house to wash his hands. The story was that he'd taken one look at Susan and then hightailed it out of there. Was her mother wrong to think that Ryan loved her as much as she loved him?

"It's just a name from my mother's past. It is, uh, it was...an old love."

Julia didn't know what to do. Chances were that when Susan regained consciousness, she would start babbling about how she had known all along that Ryan wasn't dead and Julia couldn't let that happen. If word got back to the originator of the contract that Ryan was still alive, the nightmare chase would start all over again. Right now, according to what Susan had been told, they thought that Ryan was dead, and she had to make sure it stayed that way.

"Officer Allen, could I please have a private moment with my mother?"

"You want the medical team to leave the room?"

"Just for a minute. Please."

Officer Allen shrugged, went into the room where Susan was stretched out on a cot, and said a few words to the responders.

"You her daughter?" one of them asked.

Julia nodded. "Is she going to be all right?"

"Looks like she's coming around."

When the room was cleared, Julia leaned over her mother. "Mom, can you hear me? Mom?"

Susan struggled to open her eyes. "Ryan, he's here! Keith Lambert is really Ryan! He's here in town! I told you he wasn't dead. He's here…."

"Listen to me, Mom. Listen! Keep your mouth shut about Ryan. Did you hear me? Don't say his name."

"Ryan's alive!" Susan cried.

Julia put her hand over her mother's mouth. "Be quiet, Mom! Don't say his name. The last thing you want is to get the contract people back on his trail. They think he's dead!"

The confusion in Susan's eyes cleared. "Oh, hi, Julia. Why are you here?"

"Officer Allen called me. Mom, you heard the name Charles Holiday and you passed out."

Swinging her feet off the cot, Susan stood up, and laughing hysterically, she cried, "He's in town. Oh, thank you, God! "

"Mother, just having the name Charles Holiday does not make him your former customer. Don't get your hopes up for nothing!"

"It's *not* nothing! Today, when I saw just the back of Keith, I thought it was Ryan. Keith is Ryan! I know it!"

"Officer Allen said you were trying to find your buyer to ask him a question."

"Yes. The question was about the present he'd left for me on my desk."

"What did he leave you?" Julia raised her eyebrows.

"He left me the dog collar that has been lost ever since you changed Strabismus' collar."

Julia sucked in a breath. "You've got to be joking! Where has it been, how did he get his hands on it, and what made him think it would be a good present to give to you?"

Susan almost laughed. "Keep those questions in mind and let's go find the man! In the meantime, I'll tell you the story behind the collar. Believe me, that collar is no ordinary collar!"

"Are you sure you're really all right?" Julia asked. "The ambulance is parked outside waiting to take you to the hospital."

"The hospital? I don't have time to go to the hospital!"

"Well, you'd better talk to the medical team in the next room."

"Oh, my! Did someone call 911?"

"Of course they did! You wouldn't wake up!"

Susan snatched up her purse, pushed open the door, and grabbed her daughter's hand. "Let's see how fast we can get rid of them. We have work to do! Oh, don't forget Strabismus."

***

For the rest of the day, Julia and Susan looked for Ryan. They found the café where he ate breakfast, they found the shop where he bought his clothes, they found the tailor who had made those clothes fit, but they didn't find Ryan. They talked to the clerk at the motel checkout desk about the last time she had seen Charles Holiday. All she could tell them was that when he pulled his car up to the front office to come in and settle his account, the car had been packed. What direction had he gone when he pulled out, they asked. North, she said.

That was the sum total of the clues they'd unearthed after four hours of work. Julia had to go to school the next day, so from here on, Susan was on her own.

***

The next morning, Susan woke up to a quiet house. Strabismus had gone to school with Julia, and with no one around to see her, Susan fell apart. Repeatedly, in her mind, she pictured all the contact she had with Keith Lambert. He'd even asked her out to dinner, and it hadn't seemed important enough for her to give it a second thought. The new house on the market that he called her about wasn't even close to what he'd told her was important. Did he pretend that he wanted to see it just to be with her? And she had rebuffed, ignored, and dismissed every effort he had made.

In the middle of berating herself, she paused and thought in a different direction. Why was she taking all the blame? He could have told her who he was. It was as simple as that. But he hadn't. Maybe he was he having second thoughts about wanting to see her. How embarrassing would it be to find out that he really didn't want to be with her? Could her memories of the Incident be that wrong?

The Collar

***

Three days later, she was exhausted. There was no new ground to cover, no new people to talk to and there was no sign of Ryan. It was while she was stopped for a red light that she realized she was in the area of the motel where the police had said he'd stayed. For no apparent reason, she pulled into the parking lot. Staring at the units' doors wasn't going to make them talk to her; in fact, it was even silly to be here. About to drive away, the door of a unit opened, and a woman carrying a vacuum stepped out.

Susan got out of the car and approached her. "Pardon me, but do you remember the tall white-haired man who stayed here until recently?"

The woman grinned. "I sure do!"

"I'm trying to find him. I don't suppose you have any idea where he went when he checked out?"

"Well, of course I do!"

Susan's mouth dropped open. "You do?"

"We talked about it for days! He went to Mackinac Island."

"Mackinac Island?"

"He asked me if I had ever been there, and I told him that I used to work at the Grand Hotel. He asked me a million questions!"

"Did he say how long he was going to stay?" Susan asked.

"No, he didn't. I do believe he was hurting, you know, a matter of the heart? Things were not going well, he told me."

Susan thought for a moment. "Just how do you get to the island?"

"You mean you've never been there?"

"Oh, I went there on a grade school field trip, but I don't remember much about it."

The woman looked closely at Susan. "Lordy, lordy! I'd bet my last dollar that you're the woman that's been giving him heart trouble!"

Chapter 28

A despondent Ryan had checked out of his motel room, filled his car with gas, and headed north. One look at the map revealed there were two possible ways to get to Mackinaw City where he would catch a ferry to Mackinac Island. The scenic way would be the one that hugged the shore the whole way north to Petoskey before it headed inland. The other route was probably a few more miles, but when he saw that I-75 went straight to Mackinaw City, he turned east until he hit it, turned north, and set his speed control at 70. The two things that he didn't need right now were scenery and being pulled over for speeding.

The Susan thing wasn't working the way he dreamed it would; she wasn't attracted to him at all. In fact, she dismissed him as if he weren't important. He needed to get away and rethink the problem. If he couldn't get her to fall in love with Keith Lambert, then he had to come up with a way of presenting himself as Ryan without shocking her too badly. A few days away might do him some good. Anyhow, he'd always wanted to visit Mackinac Island because of its uniqueness. The tales the cleaning woman told him and the description of the island in the brochure had captured his interest. The island, it stated, sits in the Straits of Mackinac at the point where Lake Huron joins with Lake Michigan. The island is just three miles from the southeastern end of Michigan's Upper Peninsula and is accessible only by ferryboat or plane. Once on the island, transportation is by foot, bicycle, or horse-drawn carriage. How could you not want to visit such an enchanted place? He hadn't made a reservation, but with luck, maybe he could stay at the Grand Hotel. The brochure had pictures of the 660-foot-long front porch that looked out over the Straits of Mackinac.

It was a two-and-a-half hour trip to Mackinaw City where he parked his car and boarded the ferry for the island. As the ferry neared the island, from the deck he caught a glimpse of the Grand Hotel looking large and stately on the side of a bluff.

After the short three-mile boat ride, Ryan landed on the historic island. What surprised him the most was the smell of horse manure that hung like a malodorous cloud over the downtown area. As he waited to cross the street, one of the horses pulling the passing carriage urinated. Fascinated by the river of pee that was running his way, he quickly realized that unless he jumped back onto the sidewalk, his shoes were about to be soaked.

The brochures were right. Mackinac Island certainly was unique.

Ryan looked out the window of his room at the Grand Hotel and was pleased to see the sun shining on boats of all sizes and shapes as they moved effortlessly through the water. He was trying to picture what the harbor would be like in the long Michigan winter when the island was surrounded by ice, when the thought that Susan should be here looking out the window with him brought his dilemma to mind. She wasn't here because his stupid plan hadn't worked.

His empty stomach rumbled to remind him that if he wanted to eat in the dining room of the Grand Hotel, according to the brochure, he had to be formally dressed. For the next couple of hours, he walked along the main streets of the island, found a great clothing store, visited delightful shops, and ate a huge chunk of Mackinaw fudge.

Dinnertime found him wearing his new outfit but without an appetite. He was debating skipping dinner when the chatter of a couple caught his attention. Seeing that he was alone, they invited him to share their table. Their enthusiastic accounts of their sailing adventures held Ryan's interest as servers kept their wineglasses brimming and the breadbasket full.

Through the appetizer, the couple took turns describing what it was like to be on the island for the finish of two races, each within a week of each other in July, that brought to the island over five hundred boats along with over three thousand sailors each year. The first of the two, the Port Huron to Mackinac Race, was described between bites of prosciutto-wrapped grilled shrimp.

While they enjoyed poached salmon, asparagus and stuffed baked potatoes, stories about the parties, the food and drink that followed the Chicago to Mackinac race had people from other tables looking their way, interested in what was making the white-haired man laugh so hard.

It was when they were eating pecan pie piled high with whipped cream that the couple invited him to accompany them the next day on a short sailing trip; he eagerly accepted.

For the next three days, when he wasn't sailing with his new friends, he was exploring. While strolling through Marquette Park, he leaned his head back and looked up. Fort Mackinac, built on the 150-foot high limestone bluffs by the British in 1780, was an impressive sight. Ryan was still looking up, wondering if seeing the fort was worth the steep climb, when a chattering group of tourists, being led by a guide, passed him. The decision made, he attached himself to the group. The guide's chatter along the way was full of interesting historical facts about the fort, ending with the two strategic battles for control of the Great Lakes during the War of 1812. His ears didn't really appreciate the blast when the big gun was fired. The tour included a visit to the museum, and ended with a cup of tea at the tearoom within the fort.

Much as he was enjoying himself, watching the sailing couple exchange loving glances and touches made him envious. He needed to get back to Susan. He would find out what time the next ferry left for Mackinaw City in the morning, and he'd be on it.

The Keith Lambert plan hadn't worked. The way he felt about Susan, he knew that there was no way he would even be attracted to someone else, so why had he thought it would be any different for her? It was time to leave the island, find Susan, and clear up the whole Keith Lambert mess. Just thinking about how great their reunion was going to be made his heart sing.

His new sailing friends insisted on seeing him leave the next morning. As the last person to board the ferry to return to the mainland, Ryan turned to the wife, and in his excitement at the thought of seeing Susan, grabbed her and enthusiastically hugged her.

**

Armed with instructions from the housekeeper on how to get to the island, Susan rushed to her motel. She left Julia, who had taken the dog for the day, a message on her cell phone, and in case she'd be gone for more than a day, she grabbed an overnight bag. While throwing in a change of clothes, cosmetics and a toothbrush a sudden thought made her catch her breath. *If* she found Ryan on the island, and *if* things went the way she wanted them to go, and *if* no ferries were scheduled to return to the mainland until the next day, and *if* the two of them had to spend the night together on the island, and *if*....

Susan grabbed a black negligee, threw it into the bag, snatched her purse and car keys, and headed for Mackinaw City.

Although she'd been to Mackinac Island years ago, it was but a distant memory. The woman at the motel had spoken in length about the best way to get to the island. The route hugging the lake looked inviting if you had time to enjoy all the little towns along the way, but since she was in a hurry, she turned east until she hit I-75.

By the time she arrived at Mackinaw City, ferry service to the island was closed. She was told that she'd have to wait until seven-thirty the next morning for the first ferry of the day. The man locking up the office pointed her in the direction of the Holiday Inn.

It wasn't the fault of the inn. The room was pleasant and the bed was comfortable. The problem was Susan's eyes; they wouldn't stay closed. She spent a sleepless night, eagerly waiting for morning and the first ferry to the island.

Susan boarded the seven-thirty ferry full of anticipation and excitement that turned to a bit of apprehension as the small craft neared its destination. The island that looked like a small dot on the map was really quite large. Finding Ryan might not be easy.

From the deck of the boat, she caught a glimpse of the Grand Hotel looking large and stately on the side of a bluff. She remembered the hotel because she and several of her classmates had wanted to sit on the huge front porch but changed their minds when they found out that sitting on the porch wasn't free. One thing she knew, if she stayed overnight, it wouldn't be at the expensive Grand Hotel.

At the end of the ferry ride, Susan was standing with the other passengers waiting for the ramp to be lowered, when she noticed that another ferry was loading for the trip back to Mackinaw City. From the looks of it, there was one man who was holding up the departure. The next thing Susan noticed was the woman. Smartly dressed, slim, and extremely attractive, her arms were wound around a tall white-haired man who was hugging her as if the last thing in the world he wanted to do was leave her.

It was Ryan.

Her legs crumbled as a crushing wave of loss swept through her. The man who was standing behind her managed to catch her before she hit the deck. Pushing their way out of the crowd, he found a bench and lowered her onto it.

"Ma'am? Ma'am?" he asked. "Are you all right?"

Susan didn't want to open her eyes. In fact, she never wanted to open her eyes again. She'd just sit here forever with her eyes closed and pretend she hadn't seen what she'd seen. The truth was brutal. Ryan really wasn't hers, at least not exclusively hers. How many other Susans did he have stashed across the country? He'd played her like the fool she was.

The noise of the departing ferry roused her. Ryan was headed back to Mackinaw City, and who knew where he would go from there.

She smiled weakly at her rescuer. "Thank you so much for catching me," she said as she pushed her way off the bench and stood up. "I was never good at riding the waves, but I'm better now. Thank you again."

As soon as her feet hit the ground, she lined up for the next ferry leaving the island for the trip back to Mackinaw City.

So much for Mackinac Island and her black negligee.

CHAPTER 29

Ralph Young huddled in the corner of the sofa and watched his wife and daughter work on a thousand-piece puzzle. The invitation for him to join them had fallen on deaf ears; he had other things to worry about. Knowing that Judd Slagle would do anything to find his family, Ralph couldn't help but wonder just how safe the house really was. Three people, Officer Allen, Detective Hatch, and Ralph, just three people knew what had been in the dog's collar. A title or a uniform wouldn't stop Judd Slagle. Ralph knew that the police officer and the detective weren't any safer than he was.

Officer Allen had smoothed over his absence from the bank in such a way that Ralph ended up sounding like a hero; his job was secure. For that, he was thankful, but deep down, Ralph knew that he didn't deserve it. He hadn't lived up to his own expectations, and he'd violated the trust that the women had placed in him. Finding out that he was human destroyed the picture he had painted of himself over the years.

Soon, very soon, the directions that had been hidden inside the collar would lead them to where the women had stashed the wealth. Once it was safely deposited in the bank, the horrific drama in which he had starred as a prime character would be over.

Ralph's eyes wandered back to the clock; two minutes had passed since the last time he'd looked at it. At noon today, Officer Allen, along with Detective Hatch, bank officials, and armed guards were going to the cemetery where Minnie was buried. The message, written before Minnie's death, directed them to go to the family plot and find Minnie's tombstone. Carved on it was Minnie's date of birth and a dash. The instructions? Dig under the dash.

Because Judd had been making inquiries around town about his whereabouts, Ralph was not permitted to leave the safe house and accompany the group to the cemetery.

The ringing of the doorbell surprised Ralph. Officer Allen had promised to call the moment the stash had been exhumed, but that wasn't going to happen until noon. Few people knew his family was hidden so whoever was at his door had to be connected with the police department.

The smile of welcome on his face froze when he flung open the door. Judd Slagle took advantage of Ralph's hesitation, and in a matter of seconds, he was inside the safe house holding Ralph immobile. In a matter of minutes, Ralph and his very surprised wife were taped to chairs while Sandy, their ten-year-old terrified daughter, cried hysterically.

Judd pulled the girl to him, patted her cheek, and looked at Ralph who was wild-eyed and struggling with the tape.

"Take your hands off her!" Ralph screamed.

Judd grinned. "Such a nice looking girl you have, Ralph. Wouldn't it be a shame if something happened to her pretty face?"

Ralph's wife cried, "What in the world is going on? Who is this man?"

Judd laughed. "Oh, your husband and I are good friends, aren't we Ralphie?"

Ralph grunted.

"Mama, I'm scared!" Sandy whimpered.

"There's no reason for you to be afraid," Judd cooed, his eyes cold. "Just tell your dad to do the right thing, and I'll be out of here."

Ralph's wife looked at him with eyes that implored him to do whatever the hateful man wanted. "Please, Ralph. Do something!"

Ralph was trying to see a clock. If he could stall Judd until after the noon hour, the stash would be out of the ground and on its way to the bank.

Think of something...think of something...anything to take up time.

Ralph's terrified brain wasn't functioning. "Uh, Judd, uh, do you really want to do this?"

Judd looked puzzled. "Of course I want to do this! Why wouldn't I?"

"Because...because," Ralph's voice quivered, "what kind of a father steals from his own daughter?"

Judd grinned. "I guess you're looking at one! Now, come on, tell me what I want to know!"

Ralph tried another subject. "H...h...how did you find us?"

"That's for me to know and you not to find out," Judd jeered. "Now, Ralphie baby, I know what you're trying to do, but let's quit wasting time. Are you going to do the right thing or do I have to...."

Sandy screamed. The knife that had appeared in Judd's hands dripped with the same color of red as the blood that was running from a cut on the girl's neck.

"Shall I do it again? How deep do I have to cut before you'll tell me what I want to know? I hope you haven't forgotten the cat."

Ralph sobbed. "How can I trust you? If I tell you, then what's going to happen to all of us?"

"You have that backwards, my friend. What's going to happen if you DON'T tell me is a better question."

"Do it!" his wife shouted.

"B…b…but…."

"We are way past the 'buts', Ralphie," Judd laughed.

"Daddy!" Sandy pleaded.

Ralph lowered his head, mumbled words that sounded like a prayer, and then looked Judd in the eye. "Tell me how you're going to work this. What happens to us when I tell you what was in the collar?"

"You mean after I tape up the girl and cut your phone lines? I'll leave."

With the sound of defeat in his voice, Ralph replied, "If only I could believe you."

"Believe me! Now, we're getting somewhere! So, spit it out, Ralphie, the sooner you do, the sooner I'll be out of your hair for good. You'll never see old Judd Slagle again because once I lay my hands on that fortune, I'm out of here!"

"With no thought of what you've done to Amelia?"

"Hell, no!"

"How do you live with yourself, Judd?"

Judd didn't need to say a word; blood ran a little faster out of the deeper cut on Sandy's neck.

"Okay, okay!" Ralph cried. "You win. Even though you didn't attend her funeral, I suppose you know where your mother is buried?"

"Whooee!" Judd snorted. "So, Mr. Big-Shot Banker, who made you the official attendance-taker?"

"It was a very small funeral, Judd. The fact that her only son wasn't there was pretty noticeable."

Judd disregarded the remark with a shake of his head. "I didn't attend my father's funeral, either, so stop with the guilt trip, Ralphie, or the cut on your daughter's neck gets even deeper."

Ralph remained silent as he thought about what he was about to do. He had so admired the two women he was about to betray, but did he have a choice? Finally, after a pause to ask their forgiveness, he stated, "Find her tombstone and dig under the dash between the date of her birth and the date of her death."

"That's it?"

Not trusting his voice, Ralph just nodded.

True to his word, Judd taped Sandy to a chair, cut the phone line, and ran out the door.

No one said a word for a minute. Finally, Ralph asked, "Can anyone see a clock?"

His wife snorted. "I don't believe you! We're tied up, Sandy's neck is bleeding, and all you can think about is the time?"

"Honey," Ralph replied through clenched teeth, "at noon today, Officer Allen, bank officials and their guards are going to the cemetery to dig up the same treasure that Judd thinks is his."

"Oh."

Sandy paused in her attempt to break away from the chair. "What if they run into each other?"

Almost but not quite, a grin was trying to take over Ralph's face. "Now, wouldn't that be interesting?"

CHAPTER 30

Ryan ignored all speed limit signs on his rush back to Susan. The three days on Mackinac Island had cleared his head; he knew exactly what he was going to do the next time he saw Susan. Pretending to be someone he wasn't hadn't worked. In fact, he had to admit that it had been a dumb idea. Sure, finding out that Ryan wasn't dead was going to shock her, but he had to believe it would be a good shock. He drove past her house without even stopping when he saw that the repair activity was still going on. Thinking that there was a better chance that she was at Town and Country Real Estate office, he drove on to the office, pulled into their parking lot, and went in.

The woman at the reception desk greeted him with a smile.

"I've seen you before," she exclaimed. "Are you here to see Susan?"

"Yes, I am. Is she in?"

"No, I'm afraid she's not."

Ryan couldn't keep the disappointment out of his voice. "Do you know where she is?"

"No, I don't. In fact, no one in the office knows, either. She just seems to have disappeared."

The look on Ryan's face prompted the receptionist to add, "We did leave a message at work for her daughter, Julia. She probably knows, but she hasn't gotten back to us."

"Julia works?"

"Yes, she's a teacher at Taft School. Do you know where that is?"

Armed with a map, Ryan left the real estate office and headed for the school. It was three o'clock and the released students, along with a few teachers, poured out the door, glad to see the end of the school day. Since Ryan had no idea what Julia looked like, he studied each female face, trying to see a trace of Susan. His back was turned when a red convertible with a blonde blue-eyed young woman behind the wheel sped out of the lot and drove away.

Discouraged when he didn't find Julia at Taft School, he headed back to the motel where he had been staying before the Mackinac Island vacation and asked for his old unit. He was unlocking the door when it opened and the housekeeper stepped out.

"Well, hello there!" she greeted Ryan.

He grinned at her. "I'm back! Did you miss me?"

"You know I did!" she teased. "Did that nice lady find you?"

"A nice lady was looking for me?"

"Sure was."

"When was that?"

"Yesterday. She came here looking for you. Well, I knew you'd gone to the island, and that's what I told her."

"What did this lady look like?" Ryan held his breath while waiting for the answer.

"Tall, blonde, blue-eyed, and beautiful!"

Ryan grinned. Yeah, it was Susan. "Did she say what she was going to do?"

"She asked me how to get to the island, and I told her."

Ryan didn't like what he was hearing. "You really think she went there?"

"I'd bet my next paycheck on it," the woman chuckled. "She sure seemed anxious to find you!"

Susan was on the island looking for him. It might be days before she figured out that he wasn't there. It was times like this that he bemoaned the fact that he didn't have a cell phone. There was only one thing to do. He turned back to his car, drove out of the motel parking lot, and headed back toward Mackinaw City.

***

Because of high winds, the ferries were running behind schedule. Susan, heartbroken, agitated, impatient, and sad, paced the dock waiting for the ferry that would take her back to Mackinaw City and her car. The pain of finding that Ryan wasn't solely hers was intense. When she thought about all the anguish that she had put herself through after returning home from the Incident, she cringed. The days spent on the swing wrapped in his fur coat now seemed silly.

The three-mile trip over rough water and high waves was scary. By the time they reached shore, her stomach was upset and her legs felt like rubber. While vowing never again to ride on a ferry, she found her car and headed for home.

172

The Collar

It was late in the day when she got within her city limits. What a day! All these years of living so close to the island and never visiting it, and then, in one day, she had made the trip there, she had made the trip back and she still hadn't visited it.

Relying on the idea that Ryan would go back to the same place, she headed for the motel. As she pulled into the parking lot, the realization hit that he probably wouldn't be as glad to see her as much as she wanted him to be. If he shared his affection with other women, as she had seen him do, then he couldn't have intense feelings just for her. By the time she reached the office, she had almost talked herself out of even looking for him.

She was surprised to find the face behind the desk was a familiar one. The last time Susan had seen her, she had been carrying a vacuum cleaner. Seeing Susan's puzzled face, the woman grinned. "My husband and I own this place, and sometimes I have to wear different hats. Yesterday the cleaning lady didn't show up, and today the receptionist called in sick." Then she stated, "You didn't find him."

"No, I didn't. But how do you know that?"

"He came back here, but when I told him about you, he went back to find you."

"No!" Susan cried.

"I'm afraid it's true."

"No!" Susan repeated.

"You could call him on his cell, couldn't you?"

Susan shook her head. "He doesn't have a cell phone."

The woman raised her eyebrows. It was hard to believe that someone in this day and age didn't have a cell phone.

Susan had turned to leave when the woman slid a key across the desk.

"He's rented the unit for an indefinite period, so why don't you use it? That way you will be there when he gets back. Looks like you two have been playing tag with each other."

Susan was tired enough to think the idea was a good one. Picking up the key, she thanked the woman, and left.

CHAPTER 31

If Judd Slagle had been a loving son, and if that son had attended his parents' funerals, he would have known where to look for his mother's tombstone. But he wasn't a good son, and the cemetery with its rows and rows of monuments overwhelmed him. It had sounded so easy: find the tombstone, dig under the dash, and disappear with the treasure. Finding the tombstone had turned into a marathon event of running up one row and down another.

He was exhausted by the time he finally found a crew that was preparing a site for an afternoon funeral. One of the workers remembered where Minnie Slagle had been buried because he'd felt sad that no one from the funeral had showed up at the cemetery to watch Minnie being lowered into her final resting place.

With the directions in his head, Judd felt full of energy and renewed greed as he ran to the correct section of the cemetery. Within minutes, he found his mother's tombstone.

Chuckling to himself, he knelt down, and with a small shovel, he started to dig. The hole wasn't deep when his shovel hit pay dirt. Tossing the shovel aside, he dug with his bare hands and uncovered a sealed package. He snatched it out of the hole, clutched it to his chest, turned his face to the sky, and yelled, "YES!"

That's when he noticed a group of people heading in his direction. Did the man leading the group have on a uniform? Judd blinked his eyes and looked again. Sure enough, it was that damned redheaded cop. They weren't in a hurry, so they hadn't seen him.

Suddenly, his legs weren't tired. With the sealed package clutched under one arm, Judd Slagle took off running like the thief that he was.

***

It was exactly noon when the group, led by Officer Allen and Detective Hatch, made its way to the section of the cemetery where Minnie Slagle rested. Bank officials, along with their armed guards, followed closely behind them.

Detective Hatch was struggling to keep up with Officer Allen's long strides. "Do we really expect trouble?"

Officer Allen shrugged. "The only way our party could be crashed is if someone snitched. There are so few of us who know what was in the dog's collar, I can't see that happening."

"Ralph Young really wanted to be here today. What Judd Slagle put him though was pretty awful. He's probably at home worrying about how things are going."

Officer Allen pulled out his cell phone. "I'm calling him. The guy doesn't need any more stress than he's already had. It will do him good to know that everything is fine, so far."

After ten rings, Officer Allen hung up and called the station. "Something's not right at the Young residence. Send a team over there immediately and expect the worst."

He turned to the group following and yelled, "Speed it up! There could be trouble!"

The closer the men got to the tombstone, the faster they ran. It soon became apparent that they were too late. A discarded shovel, a pile of dirt, and a hole greeted them. Someone had beaten them to it.

Stunned, the men circled the tombstone and stared at the hole. The quiet of the cemetery was shattered by the ringing of a phone. Officer Allen grabbed his cell and listened. From watching the expressions change on his face, the men knew that he was listening to bad news. When Officer Allen ended the call, he shared two words with the group; Judd Slagle.

Detective Hatch frowned. "Only three of us knew where to dig. Where did he get his information?"

"He found the safe house. Don't ask me how, because I don't know. He taped up the Young family, cut their daughter's throat...." He stopped when he heard gasps. "Not sliced...just a shallow cut to make it bleed," he corrected. "Of course Ralph told him what he wanted to know. Wouldn't we all?"

There were murmurs of agreement.

One of the bank officials commented, "Amelia's mother and grandmother were afraid something like this would happen. Judd Slagle lived up to their worst nightmare."

"I think we're done here," Officer Allen commented as he picked up the shovel. "I'll just check the hole before I fill it in....well, will you look at this!" he grinned as he pulled a package out of the hole. "Maybe Amelia didn't lose everything after all!"

***

Later that day, Ralph Young, several bank officials, and Officer Allen crowded into a back room at the bank. Since Ralph had helped both Minnie and Anna combine their assets, he would be the one to verify how much of it Judd had stolen.

The room got very quiet when it was apparent that Ralph was finished with his appraisal.

"Well?" someone asked.

Ralph scratched his head. "I don't get it."

Officer Allen spoke up. "What don't you get, Ralph?"

"Nothing's missing!"

"That doesn't make sense. Judd must have taken something."

"But I'm telling you, everything is here!"

"Then what did Judd take?"

Ralph slapped his hand against his forehead and started to laugh. "Wait a minute!" he cackled. "You know what I think was in the top package?" Ralph stopped to wipe his eyes. When no one answered his question, he supplied the answer.

"Worthless stock."

"Worthless stock? Where would the two women have gotten stock like that?"

"Long before I met her, Minnie fell for a Ponzi scheme. Anyhow, the young man who scammed her was quite the con artist. She talked about him in such glowing terms that I do believe the old lady had a crush on him. There was nothing I could say to discourage her from believing that eventually he would make it right. She believed in him to the end."

"If you're correct, then Judd ran off with nothing but worthless stock."

178

"Looks like it," Ralph grinned. "It couldn't have happened to a nicer guy!"

CHAPTER 32

Amelia, who would never think of running in the hall, could see the tail end of the line disappearing into Miss Cook's room. Once the door was shut, she would be considered late, and that would mean a trip to the principal's office to get a late pass. This morning, the house was so quiet that she had overslept and almost missed the bus.

Seeing the door about to swing shut, she stopped, turned around, and started the much-hated trek to the office when she heard Miss Cook call her name.

"Amelia?"

Amelia turned back. Miss Cook hadn't shut the door after all. This was the first nice thing that had happened to her in days.

Julia called to her. "Good morning, Amelia!"

Amelia hesitated, and then made the decision. "Miss Cook, I need to talk to you."

Julia blinked. Something bad must have happened to change Amelia's mind. Judd hadn't yet been charged with the child-abuse claim and wouldn't be until protective services found a safe place for Amelia.

"Stay out here in the hall, Amelia. Let me get the class started on an assignment, and then I'll join you out here. Is that all right with you?"

Amelia nodded.

"It won't be more than a few minutes. I promise you."

Amelia paced back and forth. She might be making the biggest mistake of her life but she was desperate. Her dad hadn't been home in four days, she had no money, and her stomach was so empty it ached.

In a matter of minutes, Julia joined Amelia outside the room.

"Can we talk here, or would you prefer a room?" Julia asked.

Amelia didn't bother to answer the question. "Miss Cook, Dad left, and I don't think he's coming back. I have no money, and there's no food in the house."

"Oh, Amelia! Are you hungry?"

The girl nodded.

"How long has your dad been gone?"

"Four days. I liked being alone for a while. At least he wasn't around to hurt me, and to answer your question, yes, my dad hurts me. I can show you scars and new bruises if you need to see them."

Julia curbed the urge to reach out and hug the girl. She could hear her unattended class getting noisy but she couldn't shut Amelia down now that she wanted to talk.

"Who else lives in your house?"

"It's just me and my dad."

"Has he ever left you alone before?"

Amelia nodded. "Yes, but not for four days."

"Was he upset? Did you get the feeling that he was in trouble?"

"Miss Cook, my dad doesn't get into trouble; he makes trouble for other people. Whatever it was, it sure made him happy. He was laughing and talking to himself while he was throwing clothes into a suitcase, but what he was saying didn't make sense."

Julia frowned when sounds of Strabismus barking and something smashing sent the class into wild laughter. The last thing she wanted to see was Mrs. Sheldon coming down the hall with a scowl on her face.

"Amelia, I have to step back into the room and see what's going on."

She smiled the first smile of the day. "Sounds like they're having fun in there."

"Let's go in. When I get the class quieted down, I'm going to call a friend and tell him to bring you some food. Do you have a request?"

Amelia's eyes brightened. "A hamburger with cheese, bacon, pickles…just so it's big! And a Coke and french-fries…."

"Sounds wonderful!" Julia grinned. "Now let's go in and see what that big smashing noise was all about."

A subdued group of students was silently poring over their assignment when Julia turned her back and pulled out her cell phone.

Denny answered on the second ring. "Aren't you in the middle of the first period? Something wrong?"

"Good morning to you, too. Remember the girl I told you about? Amelia?"

"This is a coincidence! I have something to tell you about Amelia."

"Really?"

"Really."

"Why do you know something about Amelia that I don't?"

"Because I'm out here in the real world where things are happening and you aren't. Anyhow, I overheard a conversation between Detective Mitch and Officer Allen. But you go first."

Julia took a deep breath. "Well, she finally admitted to me that her dad hurts her. Something must have happened to change her mind about telling on him, but she did. Anyhow, seems her father has been gone for several days and Amelia is hungry. Could you please bring her something?"

"I know why her dad's gone, but let's get to the food first. Does she want anything special?"

"A Coke, French fries, and a really big burger were her requests. The burger needs to have cheese, bacon, and pickle on it. Now, what's this about her dad?"

Denny laughed. "Hon, you sure stirred up a hornet's nest when you lost the collar. Judd Slagle wanted the information that was in it, big time!"

"Get to the point! I have a room full of eighth-graders staring at my back!"

"But it's such a juicy story! I hate to leave out the details."

"Denny!"

"Okay. The message stored in the collar said to go to Minnie's tombstone and dig under the dash after the date of her birth. Remember, she was still alive when the message was written."

"That's it? That's the message?"

"Yep. Ralph was not allowed to leave the safe house where he and his family have been hiding, so just Officer Allen, Detective Hatch, a few bank officials and their armed guards went to the cemetery. When they found the tombstone, it was obvious that someone had gotten there first; there was a hole dug right under the dash."

Julie gasped.

"It's the details of the story that make the story!"

"Denny!"

"Okay. In a nutshell, Judd Slagle found the safe house, tied up the family and terrorized Ralph into telling him where the stash was buried, got to the cemetery before the good guys, dug a hole, and ran off with a package that contained worthless stock, and left behind the package that had all the goodies in it. So Amelia's wealth is safe. I'm off to Burger King. Oh, and your mother is not on Mackinac Island. I saw her going into a motel and it's not the one she's been living in while her house is being put back together. Bye."

Julia held the silent phone in her hand while she tried to sort out all the information Denny had just dropped on her. It could be good news about her mother. If she was spotted near a motel that was not the one she was staying in, it probably meant that she'd found Ryan and was staying with him at his motel. Julia smiled. It would be so good to have her mother's love life settled.

True to his word, Denny soon knocked on her classroom door. Julia motioned for Amelia to follow her into the hall.

"Amelia, take the food and go into Mr. Marsh's room. It's empty this period."

After Amelia left, Julia turned to Denny. "Why haven't the men involved in this mess realized that if Judd isn't around, then Amelia is living on her own?"

"What men are you talking about?"

"Why, Ralph Young, for one. He helped the women combine their wealth. And what was that bomb you dropped about Judd running off with worthless bonds?"

"Minnie had been scammed by a young con artist. She believed to the end that the young man liked her so much, he would make it all happen. The package Judd grabbed was that one."

"What's Judd going to do when he finds out he didn't steal anything?"

Denny shrugged. "Probably nothing good. But what are you going to do about Amelia?"

"Me? What am I going to do?"

"Yes, you. You can't allow her to be all alone when Judd finds out that he didn't get anything. I would imagine if something were to happen to her, he would get it all. For her safety, take her home with you."

"I can't do that; I'm just her teacher. But if the news gets out that no adult is living with her, Social Services will be called. Some social worker will come into my classroom and take Amelia."

"Take her where?"

"A foster home."

"You can't let that happen, and another thing, you're more than a teacher, Julia. I've heard you talking about the girl many times. Pretend that you don't know what's going on and take her home because...."

"Finish it, Denny. Because why?"

"Uh, because she won a spelling bee?"

Julia laughed. "Not a good reason. I'll come up with something. The crew manager seems to think the men will be gone out of mom's house by the end of today. If so, I could say I was taking her home for dinner."

Denny raised his eyebrows. "You know very well that there's nothing in the refrigerator in your mom's house."

"Well, there would be if you'd go to the store and buy dinner stuff."

"Such as?"

"Spaghetti? Everyone loves spaghetti, don't they?"

"I'll do it."

"Oh, and get extra. If mom and Ryan are really back together, we just might have to feed them. I'm looking forward to meeting the man who captured my mom's heart."

CHAPTER 33

The two-and-a-half hour drive north to Mackinaw City was hell for Ryan. The thought of Susan and her pointless search for him in unfamiliar hotels, restaurants, and tourist sites pushed him to challenge the speed signs. He wondered how many miles an hour over the posted signs limits could he could go without being pulled over.

Keith Lambert was the name on the identification he was carrying. It had been a gift from one of the orderlies the first time he was in the hospital. Ryan had said just enough for the orderly to sense that he could be of service to the mysterious patient. Ryan hadn't questioned the man as to how he could duplicate a key that had let him into Susan's house before he went back to the hospital, or how he could produce fake documents that could pass close inspection. He was just grateful that he could.

With the forged documents, he was able to buy a car, and when he was told that in the state of Michigan he had to go to the Secretary of State's office and obtain a certificate of insurance, he'd had just a few nervous moments. He paused to give thanks for his talented friend and for the offshore accounts that were still full from his professional golfing days.

Without a schedule, it was pure luck that he arrived in Mackinaw City in time to make the next ferry to the island. It was getting late in the day; he'd have to spend the night on the island and look for her tomorrow. He doubted very much if she'd choose an expensive hotel like the one he'd stayed in, so he wouldn't stay at the Grand Hotel. The thought of finding her before turning in for the night was an exciting one. The moment that he'd been dreaming about was actually going to happen. It was the dream that had sustained him through the beating, through all the operations and therapy sessions, and through painful sleepless nights. There had never been a moment of indecision about Susan. He remembered the moments of doubt when he was courting Laura, his ex. Was she really the one? Did he truly love her? He finally decided that she was the one, and look what happened to that union. Laura had taken up with Ted, his best friend and caddy, and worked with people to help create the contract on him. Ted found him left him for dead and probably collected the money.

Now was not the time to think of the past. Now was the time to look forward to a life of love with Susan. If he was lucky and found her in time, they could spend the night together on the island. In that case, he'd ask for the most expensive suite at the Grand Hotel.

***

Sound asleep in Ryan's bed, Susan was awakened by the ringing of her cell phone. For a brief moment after opening her eyes, she had no idea where she was. And then it all came rushing back. She was in Ryan's room. He was real, he was alive, and he was looking for her. All around her was proof that she had been right when she alone claimed that he wasn't dead.

"Hello?"

"Mrs. Cook?"

"Yes."

"This is Mike, the project manager. We're finished. All I need is your walk-through approval and then we'll be out of your hair."

"You mean right now?"

"Is that possible? The men would like to go home, but they can't go until you give your okay."

Susan thought for a minute. She hated to leave Ryan's unit before he came back, but she could leave him a note.

"I'll be there in twenty minutes."

Searching through the desk in the room, she found a pen and a pad of paper that advertised the motel. Pen in hand, she started the note.

Dear Keith, I know you are really Ryan....

No, that wouldn't do. She tore off the sheet and started another note.

Dear Ryan, I know you are not Keith....

She tore that one off.

Dear Keith/Ryan....

Wait a minute. He had kept his identity hidden from her for a reason; what that reason was, she had no idea. Maybe it would be best just to play along with him, pretend that he really was Keith Lambert, and then see how he handled the transition from Keith to Ryan.

After throwing the torn pages into the wastebasket, she grabbed her purse and ran for her car. It would feel good to be back in her own home now that it had all new furnishings; there would be no bad memories connected to the replaced items. Thank God for homeowner's insurance!

Twenty minutes later, she pulled into her driveway and was surprised to see Julia's car pulling in behind her.

Julia opened her car door and called, "Hi, Mom, did you find him?"

Susan shook her head. "We've been playing tag. I've been back and forth to Mackinac Island today, and so has Ryan. He's there right now looking for me."

"And you're sure that Keith is really Ryan?"

Susan grinned. "I *know* he's Ryan. I was waiting in his motel room, but Mike said I had to come home and give my okay on his work so the men could go home. I'd much rather have stayed at the motel."

Julia went around to the other side of her car, opened the door, and helped a young girl out.

"Mom, I've brought home a guest for dinner. Amelia, this is my mom, Mrs. Cook."

Susan's eyes widened. Were teachers allowed to bring students home with them?

"Hello, Mrs. Cook," Amelia said softly.

"I'm glad to meet you, Amelia. You are welcome to have dinner with us, but Julia, is there anything in the house to cook for dinner?"

"Mom, Denny is taking care of it."

"So Denny's a guest for dinner, too?" Susan teased.

"He's more than a guest, Mom. He's the cook."

"Well, Amelia, we're all in for a treat because Denny's a good cook. Now let's go into the house and see what the workmen have done with it."

The Collar

Susan opened the door and stepped into what looked like a new house.

"Wow!" she breathed. "Mike, at first glance everything looks marvelous. But I certainly can't take it all in with one glance. Do I have a few days of living with it before I sign off?"

"Of course. This is just a preliminary walk-through, showing you that we've cleaned up our mess and removed our equipment. Oh, and that includes inspecting the upstairs, too."

Susan nodded, and for the next ten minutes she looked, pointed, gushed, and finally said, "Mike, go home. Everything looks just wonderful, but if it isn't I'll let you know."

The noise of Mike and his crew leaving woke Strabismus who had been asleep in Julia's car.

Inside the house, Susan asked, "Is that Strabismus I hear?"

"Oh, he's still in the car," Julia said. "Amelia, would you run outside and bring him in, please?"

Amelia, glad to be asked to do something, nodded, and ran out the door.

Susan turned to Julia. "Are teachers allowed to take students home with them? Isn't it asking for trouble?"

"Mom, I brought her home for her own safety."

"Safety? Who's threatening her?"

"Her father."

"I'm missing something here," Susan confessed. "But before I die from curiosity, what was the message in the collar?"

"It said the treasure was buried in the cemetery by Minnie Slagle's tombstone, under the dash after the date of her birth."

"And was it?"

"Yes, it was, but Judd Slagle beat them to it. He'd found Ralph Young and his family at the safe house, and by threatening their daughter, found out where the treasure was buried."

When Julia's account of the story ended, Susan sat quietly for a bit, and then she asked, "So Judd has nothing?"

"That's right. Now if something were to happen to Amelia…."

Susan nodded. "I get it; Judd would get it all. Are the police looking for Judd?"

"Big time, but no one has seen him. Well, Amelia saw him when he ran home to pack a suitcase. He left her there all alone with no money and no food in the house."

"Well, I can see why you brought her home for dinner, but you can't keep her. You know that."

"I do, but as soon as it's found out that she's alone, Social Services will step in, and she'll end up in a foster home. I can't see her being safe there, either."

Susan looked around, and not seeing her dog, became alarmed. "Shouldn't Amelia be back by now?"

"Oh, God!" Julia cried as she ran out the door in time to see a car speeding away. Strabismus' empty cage was in the middle of the driveway.

"Mom!" she yelled. "Call 911! Amelia is gone!"

CHAPTER 34

Ryan banged his head against the steering wheel. He never should have taken the route home that directed him through Charlevoix; the drawbridge was up. Traffic was backed up for miles for just one sailboat that, to him, seemed to be moving through tar instead of water.

His search for Susan on the island hadn't produced even one witness who remembered seeing a beautiful tall, blonde, and blue-eyed woman. It was the beautiful part of the description that had them shaking their heads. The owner of the motel had been wrong; Susan hadn't gone to Mackinac Island.

He released a sigh of relief when the bridge was finally lowered and traffic began to move. According to the GPS screen on the dashboard, he had one more hour of driving before he'd be back at his motel. His plan was to make one quick stop to unload his car, and then he'd search for Susan until he found her. To hell with trying to soften the shock.

After parking his car at the motel, he grabbed his suitcase out of the backseat, unlocked the door to his room, and rushed in. A glance in the mirror as he was unpacking startled him. The growth on his face was much more than a five o'clock shadow and he probably needed a shower.

Fifteen minutes later, freshly showered, shaved, and wearing a clean outfit, he was about to head out the door when his eye fell on the scraps of paper in the wastebasket. Curious, he stooped and picked them up.

His hands started to shake when he realized he was holding notes that Susan had written.

Dear Keith, I know you are really Ryan....

Dear Ryan, I know you are not Keith....

Dear Keith/Ryan....

Susan had been in his room...and Susan had figured it out!

With renewed resolve, Ryan ran to his car and headed for Susan's house. Within minutes, he was driving down her street, observing the activity and wondering what was going on. He was vaguely aware that a man was pointing at him, but he didn't pay much attention until a police officer stepped into the middle of the street and flagged him down.

"That's him!" the man cried. "I recognize the white hair! That's the man, but he was in a different car when he was driving around the neighborhood like he was looking for someone! If he doesn't have the girl, I'll bet he knows where she is!"

Ryan panicked. He had no idea what was going on, but whatever it was, he knew it wasn't good. When they checked his identification and found that the person didn't exist, he'd be in a lot of trouble.

***

When the blaring of police sirens brought Susan's neighbors out of their houses to see what was causing the ruckus, it was apparent that something was going on at the Cook residence. Most of the neighbors became bored and left when nothing much happened after the police entered the house. When the uniformed cops came out of the house, the few who had stayed to watch were the first neighbors to be questioned. Had they seen a strange car in the neighborhood? Had they seen a man grab a thirteen-year-old girl?

Inside the house was a different story. Amelia was gone, probably taken by her father. However, until the police could come up with an eyewitness, that was just speculation. Julia, who had to explain to the officials why she'd brought a student home for dinner, was exhausted from crying. Susan, who wanted to go back to Ryan's motel room and wait for him, knew that leaving Julia when she was so upset was out of the question. And where was her dog? Had Strabismus been kidnapped, too?

A commotion out on the street caught her attention for a second, but when the police car drove off with a man in the back seat, she felt a bit of relief. Maybe they had made some progress in finding Amelia.

CHAPTER 35

Ryan clutched the bars on his six-by-eight cell with white-knuckled fists. Throughout the entire embarrassing incident, he hadn't uttered a single word; how long could he stay silent was the big question. Being thrown in jail was the last thing he expected to happen to him in his search for Susan. A thought that Ryan the golf pro had to stay dead in order for him to stay alive almost made him smile. That summed up his problem. The contract holder believed that Ryan the golf pro was dead. Ted, his used-to-be-best-friend and caddy, probably collected the money along with Laura, Ryan's ex-wife. If word got out that Ryan was still alive, the hide-and-seek game would start all over again; he was tired of running. The thought that Laura and Ted, who probably had already spent most of the contract money, would be in trouble sparked a short-lived flare of revenge.

His jailers had discovered that the documents he carried in his pocket were bogus. They'd questioned him for hours, but he'd remained silent. He couldn't tell just anyone why he was pretending to be someone other than himself.

The Collar

Once again, as it was when he was running for his life from the contract men, the name Susan came to him. Thinking about all the trouble he'd gotten her into that time, he tried to ignore the thought, but it wouldn't go away; if anyone could get him out of this mess, it was Susan. Dare he have his jailers call her? In all the dreams that he'd had about their reunion, not one of them had him looking at her through the bars of a jail cell.

"Anybody out there?" he called.

The only other prisoner commented, "Don't waste your breath, buddy."

"Hello!" Ryan called. "I'm ready to talk."

"I told you, save your breath. Anyway, they're all at lunch."

"No, we're not all at lunch," a voice answered. "Who wants to talk?"

"Uh, the one who is falsely accused of kidnapping someone," Ryan replied.

The other prisoner laughed. "That's what they all say."

When Officer Allen walked into the area, he looked at the two prisoners. He recognized one of them as the friendly drunk who frequently slept off his binge in the town's jail. The other one, a clean-cut handsome man with snow-white hair, looked out of place in the cramped cell.

Officer Allen stopped in front of Ryan's cell. "You haven't said a word since you were brought in. All we have on you is one man's claim that he saw you driving around the neighborhood like you were looking for someone, in this case, Amelia Slagle."

Ryan shook his head. "I have no knowledge of Amelia Slagle, and I certainly wasn't driving around looking for her."

The other prisoner snorted. "And I'm sure you have iron-clad proof of where you were for that hour."

Ryan's face lit up. Pulling his hand out of a pocket, he flashed a ferry ticket stub. "As a matter of fact I have!"

Officer Allen took the stub and looked at it. "It says that three hours ago you were in Mackinaw City. Since that means you weren't even in this area when the eyewitness said he saw you, I guess this stub is your free pass to get out of jail." Officer Allen grinned. "But I'm not letting you out until you clear up your identity problem."

Ryan's heart sank. For a moment, he had thought he'd get out of this without involving Susan, but that wasn't to be.

"For reasons that I'm not free to talk about, I can't tell you anything more. The only person who can help me is Susan Cook. Do you know her?"

"Susan the realtor? Sure, I know her. What do you want me to do?"

"Would you please call her? But don't tell her why. The world thinks I'm dead, and she's going to be shocked to see me."

"Oh, she's seen you, all right!" exclaimed Officer Allen. "You were with Susan when I found her at the Omelet Shop."

"Ah, yes. That was you. I was just about to tell her who I really am, and you took her away before I could say anything. My story is complicated and I can't tell it to just anyone. Susan knew me before I had plastic surgery, so she hasn't recognized me as someone from her past."

"I just remembered something else," Officer Allen said. "You were the one who wrapped the dog's collar and gave it to Susan as a gift."

Ryan looked puzzled. "You know about the collar?"

"That was a lot more than just a collar. Where did you find it?"

Ryan wrinkled his forehead. "Find it? Was it lost?"

Officer Allen unlocked the cell. "Come with me. Seems like you have a lot of answers to questions that need answers."

***

Susan had sat with her head on the table for so long the coffee in her cup was cold. She was exhausted; Julia had worn her out. There was no word on Amelia Slagle, and Julia blamed herself. If she hadn't brought the girl home with her....

"Julia," Susan had reasoned, "if she hadn't come home with you, she'd have gone to her own home. That would have been the first place her dad would have looked for her, so all you did was to make it a bit harder for Judd to find her. And is it really kidnapping if he was just looking for his daughter as any good father would do if she hadn't come home on time?"

"Good father? I don't think so!" Julia had replied.

"Well, think of it this way, if she had gone home after school like her father anticipated, who would have known she was missing? How long would it have been before anyone knew something was wrong?"

Julia took a deep breath, "I'm going to go to my room and lie down."

Susan hugged her. "You've worn yourself out obsessing over something that wasn't your fault. Try to sleep, honey."

Every moment Susan had spent away from Ryan's motel room had been pure torture. No doubt, he had returned from the island by now. Why was she sitting here doing nothing when he was out there somewhere?

She rushed into the bathroom, splashed water on her makeup free face, grabbed her purse, and ran out the door.

No one was around to answer the ringing cell phone that was lying on the table beside her cold cup of coffee.

CHAPTER 36

Amelia buried her face in Strabismus' fur to hide the tears that were running down her face. Her dad hated tears. It never made sense to her that when she cried because he'd hit her, he would hit her again because she was crying. She had given up trying to understand her dad a long time ago, and she certainly didn't understand why, without saying a word, he'd grabbed her as she was heading back to Mrs. Cook's house with a sleeping dog in her arms.

She was puzzled by the rough way he had thrown her and the dog into the backseat. It was almost as if he were kidnapping her, but is it kidnapping when a dad picks up his own daughter? The dog was a different matter. Mrs. Cook was not going to be pleased that, once again, Amelia had Strabismus. Right about now, the two women were going to start wondering why it was taking her so long to retrieve the dog. Would they worry about her?

The car was bumping over potholes on roads that she didn't recognize; she knew better than to ask her dad where they were going. Strabismus looked up at her from his bed on her lap, yawned and went back to sleep. Amelia wished she felt safe enough to do that, but there was something not quite right about her dad. Usually he was meticulous about his grooming, but the man who had grabbed her had an unwashed odor about him, his clothes looked as if he'd slept in them, and his unshaven face was bristly. The radio was on, but the volume was too low for her to hear what her dad was listening to so intently. Suddenly, he reached out and turned up the volume in time for her to hear the end of a police bulletin:

"….a person of interest is being held in the kidnapping of Amelia Slagle…."

"Yes!" Judd shouted.

"B…but that's not right!" Amelia blurted from the backseat.

"Just shut up," Judd snarled.

"Kidnapped? Why would people think I've been kidnapped?" She paused for a moment, and then in a hesitant voice asked, "Dad, is that what you did? Did you kidnap me?"

"I told you to shut up!" he yelled.

"You did! You kidnapped me and now you're taking me somewhere! Dad, why are you doing this?"

"Shut up!"

Strabismus stirred. The loud voices were wrecking his nap.

"Dad!" Amelia cried.

"Not another word out of you!" Judd screamed. With one hand on the steering wheel, Judd's other long, swinging arm reached into the backseat. With her seat belt fastened, Amelia felt trapped. She was bracing herself for the first blow from Judd's flailing hand when

Strabismus leaped from her lap, sank his sharp teeth into one of Judd's fingers, and held on.

Bellowing with rage while violently shaking his hand to break the dog's hold, Judd's attention was not on his driving. Since, according to Judd, only sissies wore seat belts, when the car left the road and struck a tree, his unbelted body flew out through the windshield...and then slid back in to drape over the steering wheel. After the crash, the silence was broken by one moan from Judd.

"Dad!" Amelia screamed. Unable to see what was going on in the front seat, her fingers turned to thumbs as she frantically unbuckled her seat belt. For the rest of her life, she would remember watching the blood spurt from his throat that had a shard of glass embedded in it...until it stopped. Her dad was dead.

"Dad," she whimpered.

Strabismus lay motionless on the floor of the car. Amelia, uninjured, picked up the limp dog, and crawled out. The side window was smashed, but she was able to see into the car where her dad, bloody and unmoving, was slumped over the steering wheel. Even though the smell of gasoline was strong and instinct told her that it was dangerous to stay in the area, she struggled to open the smashed car's door. When flames shot out from under the hood, she gave up, grabbed the dog, and ran. The heat from the exploding car reached them as they dashed for cover.

Amelia had no idea where she was. The road wasn't much more than a logging trail and the tall weeds that were growing inside the two tracks made it apparent that the road was seldom used. She took one more look at the burning car. To her dad, whose body was hidden by smoke and flames, she said a tearless and unemotional goodbye. Giving Strabismus a reassuring hug, she headed back the way that they had come.

CHAPTER 37

Ryan had answered all the questions that he had answers for, and since he hadn't used his forged identity to harm anyone, the police had no reason to hold him. They asked him to hang around in case Susan Cook showed up, but when she didn't, they sent him on his way. He was a free man.

The one question he had no answer for was why he had checked into the motel with a different name than the bogus one that was on his driver's license. He had made up the name Charles Holiday when he'd first contacted Town and Country Real Estate office to inquire about one of their listings. Susan had answered the phone and the rest of the story was history. The name Charles Holiday didn't mean anything to the contract people. They had found him because he had withdrawn money from an account that had Laura's name on it, so using the name had not been a dangerous thing to do; it just made him feel closer to Susan.

Susan. Where did she go after she left his motel room? Reaching into his pocket, he pulled out the three messages he had found in the wastebasket. His beautiful Susan had figured out who he was. Was she going to be angry because he had kept his identity a secret? Come to think of it, he'd even tried to get her romantically interested in Keith Lambert. Thank goodness, she hadn't fallen for that one.

He stood outside the police station and looked for his car. Not finding it, he turned and went back into the station. The last time he'd seen it, he was looking through the window of the patrol car as it was whisking him off to jail. The car was probably back on Susan's street, but it wouldn't hurt to ask the woman behind the front desk. Her one word answer to his question about his car:

"Impounded."

With instructions on what he had to do to reclaim his car, he had the woman call a cab to take him to where the city was holding it. For a fee, she told him, he could have his car back.

***

Within minutes of leaving her house, Susan pulled into the parking lot of Ryan's motel. Just imagining him opening the door when she knocked had her heart pounding, but when she pictured Ryan grabbing and kissing her, she hesitated. Maybe her exit from the house had been a bit hasty because the last time she'd seen herself in a mirror she hadn't looked very attractive. Did she want him to see her like this? Her hair was a mess, her face was void of makeup, and she couldn't remember the last time she'd brushed her teeth.

Well, it was too late to think about her grooming now. Standing in front of his door, she put a smile on her face, took a deep breath, and knocked.

Either Ryan wasn't in the room, or he was ignoring her. A picture flashed into her mind of Ryan hugging the woman at the ferry dock. What if he had her in the room with him? Fueled by instant fury, she grabbed the doorknob, turned it, and stormed in; the room was empty.

So where was he? What if he had gone to her house looking for her and she hadn't been there? She needed to call home and talk to Julia. Susan's search for her cell phone became frantic when she couldn't find it in her purse. Rushing back to her car, she looked for it in the cup-holder where she usually put it, and then she hunted for it on the floor and under the seat. A feeling of uneasiness came over her. How could she get in contact with someone if she got into trouble? What if she had a flat tire, or a problem with her car? What did people do before cell phones?

Trying to remember when she had seen it last, an image of her phone lying on the table right beside her coffee cup flashed into her mind. She crawled into her car and headed for home.

Julia's car wasn't in the driveway when she arrived back at her house. She had been sound asleep when Susan left just a short time ago, and as she pulled her car into the driveway, she wondered what had roused her daughter from her nap. Rushing into her kitchen, she skidded to a stop by the table expecting to see her cell phone right beside her coffee cup. There was neither a cup nor a cell phone on the clean table. Instead, Julia had left her a note.

Mom... Your ringing phone (that you obviously forgot) woke me. You are wanted at the police station. Mom, what in the hell have you gotten yourself into now? LOL. If you are reading this, it means I haven't found you because I'm getting in my car and driving around town looking for you. Oh, yes, I have your phone.

Julia

Susan frowned. She was wanted at the police station again? The gift-wrapped dog collar was the reason she'd been "invited" the last time. Maybe this time it was to tell her that they had found Ryan! Grabbing her car keys, she was halfway out the door when she stopped. Did she want to look this awful when she finally found Ryan?

A half-hour later, a much-improved Susan got into her car and drove to the police station. Spying a yellow cab pulling out of a prime parking spot, she waited and then quickly claimed the spot for herself.

Approaching the woman behind the front desk, Susan opened her mouth to speak and then stopped when she saw that the woman was on the phone. An impatient Susan tapped her foot until the phone call was finished.

"Yes?"

"My name is Susan Cook, and I had a mess...."

"There you are," Officer Allen interrupted her. "Better late than never."

Susan turned. "Late for what?"

"Keith Lambert, or whatever his name is, was waiting for you to show up. There's a problem about his identity, and he claims you are the only one who can explain it to us."

Susan stammered. "H...he was here? Waiting for me?"

"He was here because an eyewitness claimed he had seen Keith driving slowly around your neighborhood before Amelia Slagle was kidnapped."

"That's ridiculous!" Susan snapped. "Her father has her."

"We don't know that."

"Sure you do. But Keith, where is he?"

"Uh, probably at the impound lot paying to have his car released."

"And where is that?"

"You tell me who Keith Lambert really is, and I'll tell you where the lot is."

"I don't have time to make deals! I'll ask the front desk. And Officer Allen, you have to know that it was Judd Slagle who kidnapped his daughter!"

"No, we don't know that. And what proof do you have?"

Susan had to admit that she had no proof. "But aren't you already looking for him? Didn't he tie up the Young family, and didn't he try to steal from his own daughter?"

"Yes, he did those things, and yes, we are looking for him. But what would he gain by kidnapping his own daughter?"

"Come on! Judd has to be pretty upset about missing out on all that wealth! Who gets it all if Amelia is dead?" Susan yelled as she headed for the front desk. Over her shoulder, she added, "Lord only knows what he's doing to that child right now!"

***

"That child" was walking along the two-track road, crying and holding a limp and unmoving dog. Lost, hungry, cold, scared and with the sight of her dad bleeding out indelibly imprinted on her memory, Amelia staggered as she struggled to stay on her feet. Strabismus refused to walk, and that worried her. She could only imagine what had happened to the dog when the car hit the tree. One minute her dad was screaming and shaking his hand trying to get Strabismus to let go, and the next minute...no, she wouldn't think about that right now because she had other things to think about...like how dark it was getting and how she wished she'd had the chance to eat the spaghetti dinner. Her growling stomach woke Strabismus.

"It's going to be all right," she told the dog. "Someone is going to come along pretty soon, because," she swallowed a sob, "because they have to!"

CHAPTER 38

Ryan was not a happy man. Being thrown into jail over a false accusation was bad enough, but then finding that to get your confiscated car back you had to pay a king's ransom...whoa...he had to slam on his brakes to avoid hitting a car that had cut right in front of him. The crazy woman was driving like a maniac, but of course, there were no police around to see it. They were too busy looking for another innocent person to throw into jail, seize his car, and then make him pay to get his own car back. What a racket! Looking back through his rearview mirror, he saw the speeding car turn into the lot he had just left.

Since Ryan had nowhere to go, he drove slowly through the town. Where could Susan be? He'd heard, with his own ears, Officer Allen call her. Once he left a message, and the second time he actually talked to someone who had answered Susan's phone. Why didn't Susan have her cell phone?

Taking a chance that she might be home, Ryan drove by her house and stopped by the empty driveway. His mind took him back to the night when he had sought refuge from the contract killers by ringing Susan's doorbell. He smiled remembering their flight out the back door, their encounter with a skunk while crawling to the garage access door to her car, and their wild ride through the dark night that successfully eluded the killers. He tried to stop thinking of what happened after they crash-landed in the middle of a marijuana farm. If he thought of the wonderful things that had happened between him and Susan, then he also had to remember the absolutely terrifying experience of being beaten and left for dead.

Looking across the street, he stared at the house he had lived in for several months so that he could be near Susan. He shuddered just remembering how broken his body had been, the amount of physical therapy, and the number of operations it had taken to get him to where he was today. His incentive to work through the agony and pain was his love for Susan. Every morning when he was wheeled out to the porch, his eyes would go straight across the street to look for her. And there she'd be, sitting on the swing, wrapped in his fur coat. She'd wave to him. She couldn't have known who he was, and she never crossed the street to meet him. His arms ached to hold her. He needed to tell her that because of her, he'd never given up. But to do that, he'd have to find her. He spent a few moments berating himself for running away when Denny had taken him to Susan's house to wash his oily hand. If he had stayed, they wouldn't have been chasing each other to Mackinac Island and back.

Ryan laid his head on the steering wheel and closed his eyes. He was tired. The stress of the unexpected jail time had worn him out. If Susan were out there somewhere, he sure hadn't found her. Stifling a yawn, he turned his car around in her driveway and headed back to his motel. Maybe a nap would clear his head.

***

Susan drove out of the impound lot a lot slower than she had entered it. She wished that she could apologize to the driver she'd cut in front of, but of course she couldn't. He was out there somewhere, probably complaining to anyone who would listen about the idiot woman driver who had almost killed him. It was just that she had been in the wrong lane when the driveway to the lot had appeared sooner than she had expected. Oh, well. She'd never run into that driver again.

She had missed Ryan. Just driving around town looking for him wasn't a very good plan. While stopped for a red light, she put her head down on the steering wheel. She was tired. Honking horns from behind roused her with a start...and with an idea. The last time she had been to Ryan's motel, the door to his room hadn't been locked, but since she had never taken the key back to the office, it didn't matter. Why not go back to his room and wait for him? Eventually, he was bound to end up there.

She had just pulled into the parking lot at Ryan's motel when Julia's car skidded to a stop beside her.

Susan rolled down her window. "What's wrong?"

"I can't believe I finally found you! Mom, lock your car and come with me!"

"What's going on?"

"I'll tell you, but hurry!"

Susan grabbed her purse, locked her car, and climbed into Julia's. Before she even got her seat belt latched, Julia threw the car into gear. Without taking her eyes off the road, Julia handed her mother her cell phone.

"Here, take it before I forget that I have it. First, I want to know why the police wanted you."

"It wasn't me who was in trouble, it was Ryan; he was in jail."

"In jail? Why in the world was he in jail?"

"He must have been coming to my house because he was on our street. An eyewitness claimed he had seen Ryan driving slowly through our neighborhood for an hour before Amelia was kidnapped. That was cleared up, but then they found that the identification that Ryan was carrying stating that he was Keith Lambert was fake. He wouldn't tell them who he really is, but he claimed that Susan Cook could explain everything. That's when they tried to reach me."

Julia whipped her head around to look at her mother. "You've seen Ryan? You've actually seen him?"

Susan shook her head. "No, he was gone by the time I got there. When they arrested him, they impounded his car. He had to take a cab to the lot and pay to get his car back. I rushed to the lot, but he was already gone."

"So, what were you doing outside his motel room?"

"We keep missing each other! I figured he'd end up there at some point, so I was just going to wait there for him."

Julia sighed. "You two! You're like kids playing tag!"

"Now it's your turn. Where are we going, and why are we going?"

"Where we are going is to the area where Judd Slagle was found dead. The car hit a tree and then burst into flames."

"No!" Susan gasped.

"There was no sign of Amelia, although you and I are pretty sure it was Judd who kidnapped her and Strabismus. I haven't convinced everyone that it was Judd who took her, but there's a search party looking for her right now. But, Mother dear, you and I are going to find her before the search party does."

"Slow down! One thing at a time. So, Judd's dead? From what you've told me, he wasn't a very nice man, but he was Amelia's father. Now, she's an orphan."

"What she is now is lost! The accident killed Judd, so maybe she's out there wandering around in the woods in pain."

"You said we were going to find her before the search party. Pray tell, how do you figure we're going to make that happen? What's your plan?"

"My plan? Mother, we are going to use your dog to find Amelia."

"My dog? My dog's with her!"

"Your dog does something that no other dog does."

Susan's face brightened. "You think my Strabismus is special?"

"Mother, Strabismus is the ugliest dog I've ever seen, but what makes him special is how he responds to you when you ask a question."

"Oh."

"Just think about it! We can find Amelia if you can get him to answer to your voice. Come on! It's worth a try. It's getting dark and I know I wouldn't want to spend the night in the woods!"

"It's getting cold, too. Do you remember if Amelia had a jacket or coat on when you brought her home from school with you?"

Julia thought. "Can't say that I remember what she had on. Mom, but this is serious. The accident happened in thick woods with only two-track roads running through it."

"If the area is so isolated, how was the car found?"

"The car caught fire, and some campers noticed the smoke," Julia replied, and then she added, "I wonder why Judd was back there in the first place."

"Well, if he kidnapped his own daughter, he probably was going to hide out in the woods. Maybe there's a cabin back there somewhere."

"Think about it, Mom. If something happens to Amelia, who would get what her grandmother and mother amassed for her? He's probably so upset about losing all that wealth that he isn't thinking straight."

"Where are we going now?"

"I want to find the car and start looking from there."

"Julia, do you have a flashlight in your car? We're going to need one."

"Look in the glove compartment. There should be two in there."

They rounded a turn in the dirt two-track road and saw ahead of them a group of people milling around the remains of a scorched car.

***

The sight of a car with a real estate bumper sticker parked in the motel parking lot sent a jolt of wild expectation through Ryan. It was going to happen. Just to make sure, a peek through the car's window gave him a glimpse of a real estate sign with Susan's name on it.

"Susan is here! She's here, she's here, she's here...," he kept repeating over and over as he ran to his room, flung open the door, and stepped into an empty room.

Disappointment hit hard. That was her car out there; he'd had every right to believe she'd be in his room. So, where was she? Waves of exhaustion swept over him as he slowly removed his clothes and turned down the bed covers. He was just too tired to think. He'd figure it all out after a little nap.

CHAPTER 39

There was something wrong with Strabismus; he wouldn't walk. Amelia sighed, picked him up, and started walking again. She could picture her red-checked coat hanging on the back of a chair at the house where Miss Cook had taken her. When they'd asked her to go out to the car and bring in the dog, she hadn't put it on.

Darkness had come rapidly to the wooded area. The rutted road was so full of weeds that twice she had left the road and ended up in the woods. Both times, it had happened when there was still enough light for her to see her way back to the road.

The quiet of the woods was broken by sounds Amelia couldn't identify. Scared, cold, and hungry, she talked.

"Strabismus, do you think anyone is looking for us? I wonder how far I've walked. I think it has to be several miles. Miss Cook and her mother know we're gone, and that makes me feel a little better. I really like Miss Cook, and I think she likes me. And, Strabismus, my dad…he's dead. You didn't see what I saw, but it was pretty awful! He was a bad man, but he was my dad. How sad should I feel? I haven't thanked you for trying to protect me, so I'd do it now, but I don't know if you are even listening to me. You're so quiet it scares me, but I will thank you for your warmth. Since I can't see where I'm going, do you think we should stop walking and just wait for morning? Oh, I'm so cold! I wish you were a bigger dog so that you could warm more of me, but if you were any bigger, I wouldn't be able to carry you. Oh, did I leave the road again? I think I did. Maybe I'll stop walking...."

In the dark, Amelia didn't see the hole. It wasn't deep, but it was enough to catch her foot. A sharp pain in her ankle sent Amelia and Strabismus tumbling to the ground.

***

"I'd forgotten just how dark it gets in the woods," Susan whispered.

"And why are you whispering, Mother?"

"Maybe so I won't wake up a bear?" Susan laughed. "I don't know why I whispered. We should be yelling, don't you think?"

"Here's a plan. I'll drive for about a football field, then I'll stop and you yell, go another distance, stop, and you yell again."

Julia stopped the car and Susan crawled out. "Strabismus, can you hear meeeeee?"

Julia laughed. "Mom, that hurt my ears!"

After many stops, Susan was crawling back into the warm car when she paused and listened.

"Julia, I heard something!"

Julia climbed out of the car. "Do it again, Mom!"

"Strabismus, can you hear meeeeee?"

In the distance, a dog sang.

"That's my dog!" Susan cried. "Did you hear where it came from?"

"Ahead and off to the right," answered Julia. "Grab a flashlight, Mom!"

Stumbling along with the help from the light of two flashlights, the women worked their way to the sound of the dog responding to Susan's voice.

Finally, Amelia's cry. "Hello? Is someone out there? Hello?" added urgency to their search.

"They've got to be right here, but I don't see them."

"Looks like they wandered off the road. You'd think my dog would run out to meet me."

Following the sound, the women left the road and walked into the woods. The moving beam of a flashlight soon settled on the dog that was spread over Amelia's prone body.

"We've found them!" Julia cried.

Strabismus whined when he saw Susan, but he didn't move.

Julia ran to the girl and hugged her. "Amelia?"

"T...t...thank goodness!" Her teeth were chattering. "I'm so cold! Oh, Miss Cook! Thank goodness you found us!"

"I didn't do it all by myself. My mom helped me...well, really it was her dog."

Amelia almost smiled. "Yeah, I heard him answering your mom. Sounded like he was singing." Bursting into tears, she grabbed Julia's hand. "I was so scared! But I kept telling Strabismus that someone would find us! Oh, thank you, thank you!"

"Are you okay?" Julia asked.

"I'm awfully cold. Strabismus tried to keep me warm, but he just isn't big enough. But it's my ankle...I twisted my ankle. Do you know that my dad is dead?"

Julia paused to remove her own coat and wrapped it around the girl. "Yes, we know."

"Oh, thank you!" Amelia cried, clutching the coat. And then her face clouded. "W...who's gonna take care of me?"

"You're safe now because Mom and I are going to take care of you."

"Forever? Like live in your house?"

Mother and daughter looked at each other. What do they tell her?

"Ah, Amelia, we're not family," Julia reminded her. "You have relatives, don't you?"

"Yes, my mother's parents. But I don't know them very well. Hey, I need to tell you that there's something wrong with Strabismus. He wouldn't walk so I had to carry him."

"Did you hear that, Mom? Your dog can't walk."

"What happened?" Susan asked as she bent down and picked up her dog.

"He got hurt in the accident. In fact, he caused the accident. He bit Dad."

Susan looked alarmed.

"Well, he was protecting me. I was strapped in the back seat and Dad was trying to hit me while he was driving. That's when Strabismus grabbed his finger and hung on."

"And that's what made your dad run into the tree?"

"Yes," Amelia whispered. "Miss Cook, it was awful!"

Julia hugged the girl. "We can talk about it later, but right now we need to get you to the hospital."

"Can you carry me? I can't walk."

"Mom," Julia called. "Put your dog in the car and get back here and help me carry Amelia. I'll call Officer Allen and tell him that we found her."

CHAPTER 40

Susan kept looking at her watch; everything was taking too long. Ryan was probably back in his room by now. Or maybe he was looking for her. All of this running around playing tag with each other would never have happened if Ryan had owned a cell phone.

Amelia had been admitted to the hospital for overnight observation. With her ankle tightly taped, she'd sat up in bed and proclaimed the empty dishes on the tray had contained the best food she'd ever eaten. Her mother's parents had been notified that the granddaughter they had ignored all these years needed them. Amelia hadn't been told that she was now going to live with her grandparents. Because they had never liked the man their daughter had married, they had stayed away.

Finding an after-hours veterinarian hadn't been easy, but there is always one vet on standby in case of emergencies. When Susan and Julia finally arrived at the night's designated vet, they found Dr. Phillip waiting for them. Julia took a seat while Susan followed the vet into an examining room.

"And what have we here?" he asked.

Susan laid her dog on the table. "This is Strabismus."

The vet raised his eyebrows. "You have a cross-eyed dog?"

"Yes, I do," Susan grinned.

Dr. Phillip returned her smile. "And what is wrong with your dog?"

"For one thing, he won't walk. The car he was in hit a tree, so I imagine he got thrown around."

Susan watched the smile vanish from the vet's face. The way his eyes kept glancing at her while he was examining the dog was making Susan nervous.

Finally, she asked, "Something wrong?"

Dr. Phillip shrugged. "I've seen this dog before. How long have you had him?"

"Not very long. Strabismus was a dog that was abandoned in one of my real estate listings."

Dr. Phillip held a light up to Strabismus' eyes. "Really? I see so many dogs that are just…dogs. But then there are some that once you see them, you don't forget them. I wish I could remember…."

"Did the dog you are trying to remember have crossed eyes?"

"Yes, but that's not that unusual. It just means that the animal has weak eye muscles. I'm trying to remember who owned the dog."

Dr. Phillip spent time prodding and poking Strabismus. "I would like to keep the dog overnight so that I can take x-rays tomorrow. I don't like the looks of his left hind leg."

Strabismus' wandering eyes looked up at Susan. She was surprised at the strong bond she was feeling for the little dog. Seeing Susan's hesitation, the vet hastened to add, "The technicians will be in at eight, and I'll make sure Strabismus is the first patient they see."

"I suppose, if I have to, I can leave him."

"Ah, Mrs. Cook, I don't imagine you have medical records on your dog."

"No, I don't."

"Bringing an unprotected dog into my hospital exposes all my patients."

The dog turned his eyes from Susan to the vet. "I can see that your dog is well named," he chuckled. The expression on his face changed. "Minnie Slagle! The name just popped into my head. Minnie Slagle owned this dog!"

"That's right! It was Minnie's dog that Ralph Young locked...."

"What?"

"Ah, forget what I just said. Do you have records on the dog?"

"I should. I do believe Minnie called him Lover Boy. As I remember, she loved her dog. How did he end up in one of your listings?"

"Minnie died and the man she left her dog with didn't like him."

"Oh."

"Things happen, Doctor. About the records...."

"Let me check."

When the vet returned to the office, he was holding a file.

"Looks like Lover Boy is all caught up with his shots."

Susan laughed. Reaching over, she put her hand on the dog's head. "Strabismus, should I change your name to Lover Boy?"

Strabismus' eyes struggled to land on Susan when he heard his old name. In his excitement, he sang a few lines and part of the chorus of a song.

The vet's reaction was immediate. "What in the world was that?"

"Strabismus is a special dog. That's the sound he makes when my voice goes up at the end of a sentence."

"Just you?"

When the dog didn't react to the vet's question, Susan grinned. "Did that answer your question?"

Strabismus sang and Dr. Phillip laughed.

"You might read in the paper tomorrow how this dog helped us find a lost girl today."

"How did he do that?"

"He happened to be with the girl. I kept yelling a question until we could hear Strabismus answering. The girl sprained her ankle and couldn't walk any further."

"So I have a famous patient!" Dr. Phillip chuckled. Handing her a card, he said, "Call around noon tomorrow, and I should be able to tell you more about your dog. Oh, another thing. If you're going to keep the dog, he will need to be licensed. The forms are on the receptionist's desk on your way out."

Susan grabbed the form, and rushed into the waiting room where she found Julia sound asleep.

Touching Julia's shoulder, Susan spoke softly. "Wake up, Hon. My car is back at Ryan's motel. Let's go!"

***

Susan's hand slipped into her pocket and clutched the key to Ryan's room. As she watched Julia drive away, she was seized by unexpected panic. The key in her hand would reunite her with the man who held the power to destroy her. Was she ready for a world of hurt if things didn't work out with him? She'd dreamed, longed, and yearned to be with Ryan, to love him for the rest of her life. She had convinced herself that life without him wasn't worth living. But what if the depth of Ryan's feelings for her only existed in her imagination? What if, after they got together, she discovered that he really didn't want her as much as she wanted him?

After all this time, after surviving the deep dark periods of depression, after enduring all the ridicule that had been heaped upon her because she refused to accept the idea that Ryan was dead, did she have the courage to find out if the memories were real? Had she, over time, expanded those memories because she needed to feel loved? Could she face a colorless life without those memories?

Susan began to shake. Her feet refused to move. The key became heavy in her hand, and finally deciding that the unknown should remain unknown, she dropped the key back into her pocket and ran for the car.

The memories were too important; she just couldn't risk losing them.

Inside the room, Ryan had heard a car pull into the lot, and as he watched from his window, he saw Susan crawling out of a car that then drove away. His heart beat wildly in anticipation of their reunion. Now that Susan knew his true identity, their love for each other would be as strong as it was when they huddled together under the coat.

He felt as excited as a kid on Christmas morning. This was the woman he had been obsessing about. This was the woman he wanted to love and cherish for the rest of his life. This was the wo….

With his heart not believing what his eyes were seeing, he watched his Susan turn around and run to her car.

CHAPTER 41

Julia was so sure that her mother would spend the night with Ryan, the noise of a key opening the front door accompanied by Strabismus' warning bark was a welcoming sound. Since Denny was the only other person who had a key, that meant he was coming back to apologize. Well, she had to admit, he had the right to be angry with her. That she hadn't included him in the search for Amelia was bad enough, but the fact that she hadn't even called from the hospital or the veterinary office pushed him over the edge. He'd been left out, and it hurt. Heated words were exchanged, and soon the situation deteriorated into an all-out, "Well, what about the time you…."

Julia got to the top of the stairs in time to see that it was her mother and not Denny who had unlocked the door. She watched her mother ignoring her dog's frantic welcome as she listlessly removed her coat and threw it over a chair.

"Mother!" a disappointed Julia cried, "Why are you here? Wasn't Ryan at the motel?"

"I don't want to talk about it," Susan mumbled.

"He wasn't there?"

"Julia, I said I didn't want to talk about it!"

"But, Mother!"

"You heard me. Go back to bed and leave me alone."

Remembering the months that Susan had spent in deep depression, Julia had a premonition that those times were about to be repeated.

***

Ryan was devastated. Watching Susan drive away felt as painful as any of the surgeries or therapies he had endured. What had he done wrong? Was his pretending to be Keith Lambert the reason that she stopped loving him?

She had rejected him, and he had to leave. Just being in the same town with her would keep reminding him that she was here, but not with him.

After throwing his things into a suitcase, he headed to the office and checked out.

Within minutes after Susan's rejection, he was in his car, driving out of town.

CHAPTER 42

The pillow over her head muffled the sounds of her mother's sobs, moans, and whimpers but Julia found sleep impossible. The exciting events of the day were enough to keep her awake, but the spat with Denny was the worst. Words that had been said in anger could not be taken back. Denny had been right. She hadn't included him in the hunt for Amelia, and that's what was keeping her eyes from closing. Was it the feeling of guilt that had caused her to say all those hurtful words? Would Denny ever forgive her?

The pillow trick, while not perfect, was working so well, she almost missed her mother's gentle knock on her door.

"Julia?" her mother whispered.

Silence.

"Julia?" Susan knocked louder.

"Mom?"

"Could I come in…please?"

"The door's not locked."

When the door opened, the light from the hall fell upon the form of a devastated woman standing in the doorway. Whatever happened at the motel had destroyed her strong and beautiful mother.

Julia rubbed her eyes and sat up. "Are you here to tell me what happened?"

"Nothing happened," was the listless reply.

"Why didn't it happen?"

"I got cold feet."

"What?" Every vestige of sleep left Julia's body. Swinging her legs off the bed, she stood up. "Wait a minute, Mom! You've pined over him ever since you came back from the Incident."

Susan hung her head. "What if…what if I imagined our relationship was more than it really was?"

"Mother, where is this nonsense coming from?"

"It's not nonsense! What if," Susan paused.

"Come on, Mom, finish it. What is this big 'what if'?"

"Julia, what if our emotions were created by the highly stressful situation we were in?"

"Mother!"

"Think about it, Honey! What Ryan and I think we feel for each other could be a fantasy."

"The plane crash was a fantasy? You and Ryan hiding in a tree to escape getting killed was a fantasy?"

"That's not what I said! Those things happened. But what if the adrenaline caused by our fear exaggerated our emotions?"

"I don't believe this! You became a hermit, you quit working, and your depression was so black it scared me. And then he came back, and now you're standing here telling me that you've changed your mind about Ryan?"

"Would you listen? Did you hear me say I'd changed my mind about him? Because I didn't say that. It's just that…"

"Just what, Mother! Just what?"

"It's just that…." Susan's eyes closed and her arms crossed over her chest as if she were protecting herself. "It's just that he has the power to destroy me."

"Destroy you? What would make him want to destroy you?"

"Oh, he wouldn't do it on purpose. He'd just quit loving me when life became, you know, like…."

"Finish it, Mother! Like what?"

Susan's voice was quivering. "Like normal. Like…dull."

"What kind of convoluted reasoning got you to this point, Mom? When you love someone completely, you do expose yourself to all kinds of pain. And you're right, the person that you love has the power to destroy you, but that person also has the power to give your life meaning."

"It's the memories, Julia. If I walk away now, I'll always have the memories."

There was disgust in Julia's voice. "Mother, I watched you struggle to keep it together after Dad died, and I thought you were the strongest woman in the whole world. What happened to you?"

Susan shrugged. "Reality happened. I loved your father, and he left me, didn't he?"

"Yes, and I remember you grieved for a long time, but his dying didn't destroy you. It made you stronger."

"Oh, Honey! I didn't want it to end like this. I anticipated seeing him again so much as Ryan and not Keith. But when I thought that it might not be as grand as I dreamed it was going to be, well, I walked...no, I ran away."

"Do you think Ryan saw you?"

"Why would he have seen me? I didn't go to his room."

"So he has no idea that you are going through this...this...ridiculous doubting phase?"

"I guess not."

"Mother, go make yourself beautiful and get back to the motel right now! I don't want to see your face anytime soon. Just go!"

With renewed excitement, Susan did what Julia instructed her to do. Within the hour, she found herself outside Ryan's unit with the key in her hand. Should she knock and wake him up, or should she just quietly enter his room, remove her clothes, and crawl into bed with him? The thought of feeling his warm bare skin made her hand shake.

Once in the dark room, it was hard for her to see, but because she had been in the room before, she knew where to find the bed. Her clothes made no noise as they dropped to the floor. He was going to be so surprised when he woke up and found her in bed with him.

Strange. There was no warmth in the bed, only the feel of cold sheets. When her reaching arms encountered empty air, she jumped out of bed and turned on the light.

The bed was empty.

The room was empty.

Ryan was gone.

CHAPTER 43

Ryan had nowhere to go. How do you heal a broken heart when you have no one to listen to your tale of woe? The closest people he had as friends were back at the hospital where he had spent so much time putting his body back together. It had sounded like a good plan, but once he got there, he found that the people who had worked with him were now dealing with new patients and really didn't have time to listen to him. He thought of making another trip to Mackinac Island, but the memory of horse urine running over his shoe was enough to cross off that idea.

With nowhere to go and nothing to do, he thought constantly of Susan. Some days, he wondered if he wanted her because he had no one else. But those thoughts were quickly smothered by the loop of loving memories that kept running through his head. Susan didn't want him, but he couldn't stop loving her.

Months went by. The days were empty, and trying to fill them with activity was exhausting. How he longed to get back to the game of golf! His whole life had been centered on a game that he could no longer play. Because of his unique swing, he couldn't chance hitting a bucket of balls.

The last thing he wanted to do was call attention to himself; the contract holders thought he was dead, and he wanted to keep it that way. All he had left of his glory days when he was the king of the golf course were memories and healthy offshore bank accounts.

One morning he finally admitted to himself that he'd never actually heard Susan say the words that she didn't want him in her life. He had just seen her run away from the motel. At the time, the thought of confronting her, only to be rejected again, had been too painful even to consider. Without giving her a chance to explain, he had packed up and left.

What if?

Was he strong enough to live through another rejection?

***

Wrapped in Ryan's fur coat, Susan had reverted to sitting on the swing with Strabismus on her lap. Anger at herself for throwing away her chance for happiness made her as prickly as a porcupine. She didn't have to ask to be left alone; no one wanted to be around her. Because she didn't even try to go to work, Julia's paycheck was the only source of income again. How could she save money for a wedding if her mother never went back to work? Denny was finally selling houses, but since real estate is such an iffy occupation, they couldn't depend on it.

Time went by, and nothing changed. Fall turned into winter, and winter came and went. Finally, the warm days of spring melted the last piles of dirty snow in Susan's neighborhood. Soon the trees would be budding, the birds would be building nests, and the brutal winter would be talked about in the past tense.

While wrapped in the coat, Susan and her dog sat on the porch and watched with detached interest as a for sale sign appeared on the yard across the street. Gone was the competitive feeling that she used to have when a realtor other than herself obtained the listing of a neighbor's house. However, when in a few days a big red SOLD was slapped on the sign, she did have a moment of guilt. What she was doing wasn't fair to Julia. Her daughter had her own life to live.

Days passed, and finally a big moving van pulled into the driveway of the house across the street. As she watched the stream of men carrying furniture into the house, thoughts of the man who had lived there before had her wondering what had happened to him. She had seen the empty wheelchair being pushed into the van the night the house had been emptied. From that, she had concluded that the invalid had died. Once again, she felt bad that she had never made it across the street to meet him.

Julia was already in bed; the house was quiet. There had been a time when Susan was eager for bedtime because her nights had been filled with wonderful dreams. But the dreams had stopped. With no dreams to look forward to, she was reluctantly headed for her bedroom when she glanced out the window. A man was standing in front of a lighted window in the house across the street. Probably the new owner, she thought. Before falling asleep, she made a promise to herself that this time she wouldn't stop in the middle of the street. This time she'd cross it and meet her new neighbor.

When Susan woke up the next morning, she couldn't explain why she felt so good until she remembered she had dreamed last night. And it had been a good dream. Ryan was in it, and the love she'd felt radiating from him had been wonderful.

Oh, for another chance!

Along with the coat and her dog, Susan had just taken her seat on the swing when her attention was drawn to the house across the street. Last night Susan had seen someone's silhouette in front of a window, so it wasn't a surprise when the front door opened and a man walked out. She watched as a white-haired man walked slowly to the edge of the porch. Her breath caught in her throat. The man waved.

Susan's heart stood still. Could it be? Hope that had died the night in the empty motel room came alive and filled her. Was she going to get another chance? Strabismus grunted his displeasure when he and the fur coat were shoved aside.

The man didn't move until Susan stood up. Matching her steps, he walked when she walked, he paused when she paused, and when she stopped he stopped.

Finally, ten feet separated them. She could feel his eyes burning into hers.

"Ryan?"

He nodded.

For a moment they stood still, knowing that the end of their story was about to be written.

Ryan's heart was threatening to jump out of his chest. Paralyzed with the fear that Susan was going to reject him again, he didn't move.

Susan hesitated before she took another step.

"Susan?" His eyes searched her face.

Susan's mouth moved, but no sound came out.

Ryan quit breathing. Dear God! Was she trying to find the words to reject him again? This was it. The final rejection. His only defense against the pain that would follow was to close his eyes.

"Ryan, m…may I please have another chance?"

His eyes flew open.

He breathed. With a face that was glowing, and with eyes that were shining with love, he opened his arms.

They met in the middle of the street.

www.ingramcontent.com/pod-product-compliance
Lightning Source LLC
Chambersburg PA
CBHW030111260626
47156CB00008B/2610